**pick-
up**

pick-up

charles willeford

VINTAGE CRIME / **BLACK LIZARD**

vintage books • a division of random house, inc. • new york

First Vintage Crime/Black Lizard Edition, October 1990

Copyright © 1967 by Softcover Library, Inc.

Library of Congress Cataloging-in-Publication Data
Willeford, Charles Ray, 1919–1988.
Pick-up/by Charles Willeford.
p.   cm. —(Vintage crime/Black Lizard)
Reprint. Originally published: 1967.
ISBN 0-679-73253-5
I. Title.   II. Series.
PS3545.I464P54   1990
813'.54—dc20   90-50254   CIP

Manufactured in the United States of America
10 9 8 7 6 5 4 3 2 1

pick-
up

enter madame **1**

It must have been around a quarter to eleven. A sailor
came in and ordered a chile dog and coffee. I sliced a bun,
jerked a frank out of the boiling water, nested it, poured a
half-dipper of chile over the frank and sprinkled it liberally
with chopped onions. I scribbled a check and put it by his
plate. I wouldn't have recommended the unpalatable mess
to a starving animal. The sailor was the only customer, and
after he ate his dog he left.

That was the exact moment she entered.

A small woman, hardly more than five feet.

She had the figure of a teen-age girl. Her suit was a blue
tweed, smartly cut, and over her thin shoulders she wore a
fur jacket, bolero length. Tiny gold circular earrings clung
to her small pierced ears. Her hands and feet were small,
and when she seated herself at the counter I noticed she
wasn't wearing any rings. She was pretty drunk.

"What'll it be?" I asked her.

"I believe I need coffee." She steadied herself on the stool
by bracing her hands against the edge of the counter.

"Yes, you do," I agreed, "and you need it black."

I drew a cupful and set it before her. The coffee was too
hot for her to drink and she bent her head down and blew
on it with comical little puffs. I stood behind the counter
watching her. I couldn't help it; she was beautiful. Even
Benny, from his seat behind the cash register, was staring at
her, and his only real interest is money. She wasn't nearly
as young as I had first thought her to be. She was about
twenty-six or -seven. Her fine blonde hair was combed
straight back. Slightly to the right of a well-defined
widow's-peak, an inch-wide strip of silver hair glistened,
like a moonlit river flowing through night fields. Her oval

3

face was unlined and very white. The only make-up she had on was lipstick; a dark shade of red, so dark it was almost black. She looked up from her coffee and noticed that I was staring at her. Her eyes were a charred sienna-brown, flecked with dancing particles of shining gold.

"This coffee is too hot." She smiled good-humoredly.

"Sure it is," I replied, "but if you want to sober up you should drink it hot as you can."

"My goodness! Who wants to sober up?"

Benny was signaling me from the cash register. I dropped my conversation with the girl to see what he wanted. Benny was a flat bald, hook-nosed little man with a shaggy horseshoe of gray hair circling his head. I didn't particularly like him, but he never pushed or tried to boss me and I'd stuck it out as his counterman for more than two months. For me, this was a record. His dirty eyes were gleaming behind his gold-rimmed glasses.

"There's your chance, Harry!" He laughed a throaty, phlegmy laugh.

I knew exactly what he meant. About two weeks before a girl had entered the cafe at closing time and she had been pretty well down on her luck. She'd been actually hungry and Benny had had me fix her up with a steak and french fries. Afterwards, he had made her pay him for the meal by letting him take it out in trade in the kitchen.

"I don't need any advice from you," I said angrily.

He laughed again, deep in his chest. "It's quitting time. Better take advantage." He climbed down from his stool and walked stiffly to the door. He shot the bolt and hung the CLOSED sign from the hook. I started toward the kitchen and as I passed the woman she shook her empty cup at me.

"See? All finished. May I have another?"

I filled her cup, set it in front of her and went into the back room and slipped into my tweed jacket. The jacket was getting ratty. It was my only outer garment with the exception of my trenchcoat and I'd worn it for more than two years. The elbows were thin and the buttons, except one, were missing. The gold button was the top one and a coat looks funny buttoned at the top. I resolved to move it to the middle in the morning. My blue gabardine trousers hadn't been cleaned for three weeks and they were spotted here and there with grease. I had another pair of trousers in my room, but they were tuxedo trousers, and I used them on waiter and busboy jobs. Sober, I was always embarrassed about my appearance, but I didn't intend to stay sober very long. I combed my hair and I was ready for the street, a bar and a drink.

She was still sitting at the counter and her cup was empty again.

"Just one more and I'll go," she said with a drunken little laugh. "I promise."

For the third time I gave her a cup of coffee. Benny was counting on his fingers and busily going over his receipts for the day. I tapped him on the shoulder.

"Benny, I need a ten until payday," I told him.

"Not again? I let you have ten last night and today's only Tuesday. By Saturday you won't have nothing coming."

"You don't have to worry about it."

He took his copy-book from under the counter and turned to my page. After he entered the advance in the book he reluctantly gave me a ten dollar bill. I folded the bill and put it in my watch pocket. I felt a hand timidly tugging at my sleeve and I turned around. The little woman was looking up at me with her big brown innocent eyes.

"I haven't any money," she said bitterly.

"Is that right?"

"Not a penny. Are you going to call a policeman?"

"Ask Mr. Freeman. He's the owner; I just work here."

"What's that?" Benny asked, at the mention of his name. He was in the middle of his count and didn't like being disturbed.

"This young lady is unable to pay for her coffee."

"Coffee is ten cents," he said firmly.

"I'll tell you what, Benny. Just take it out of my pay."

"Don't think I won't!" He returned to his counting.

I unlocked the door, and the woman and I went outside.

"You're a free woman," I said to the girl. "You're lucky that Benny didn't notice you were without a purse when you came in. Where is your purse, by the way?"

"I think it's in my suitcase."

"All right. Where's your suitcase?"

"It's in a locker. I've got the key." She took a numbered key out of the pocket of her fur jacket. "The main trouble is that I can't seem to remember whether the locker's in the railroad station or the bus station." She was genuinely puzzled.

"If I were you I'd look in the bus station first. You're quite a ways from the railroad station. Do you know where it is?"

"The bus station?"

"Yes. It's seven blocks that way and one block that way." I pointed down Market Street. "You can't miss it. I'm going to have a drink."

"Would you mind buying me one too?"

"Sure. Come on."

She took my arm and we walked down Market. It was rather pleasant having a beautiful woman in tow and I was glad she had asked me to buy her drink. I would never have asked her, but as long as she didn't mind, I certainly didn't mind. I shortened my stride so she could keep up with me and from time to time I looked down at her. Gin was my weakness, not women, but with a creature like her . . . well, it was enough to make a man think. We were nearing the bar where I always had my first drink after work and my mind returned to more practical things. We entered, found seats at the end of the bar.

"Say," she said brightly. "I remember being in here tonight!"

"That's fine. It's a cinch you were in some bar." The bartender knew me well, but his eyebrows lifted when he saw the girl with me.

"What'll you have, Harry?" he asked.

"Double gin and tonic." I turned to the girl.

"I'd better not have a double. Give me a little shot of bourbon and a beer chaser." She smiled at me. "I'm being smart, aren't I?"

"You bet." I lit two cigarettes and passed her one. She sucked it deeply.

"My name is Harry Jordan," I said solemnly. "I'm thirty-two years of age and when I'm not working, I drink."

Her laugh closely resembled a tinkling bell. "My name is Helen Meredith. I'm thirty-three years old and I don't work at all. I drink all of the time."

"You're not thirty-three, are you? I took you for about twenty-six, maybe less."

"I'm thirty-three all right, and I can't forget it."

"Well, you've got an advantage on me then. Married?"

"Uh huh. I'm married, but I don't work at that either." She shrugged comically. I stared at her delicate fingers as she handled the cigarette.

The bartender arrived with our drinks. Mine was good and cold and the gin taste was strong. The way I like it. I love the first drink best of all.

"Two more of the same," I told the bartender, "and see if Mrs. Meredith's purse was left here, will you?"

"I haven't seen a purse laying around. Are you sure you left it in here, miss?" he asked Helen worriedly.

"I'm not sure of anything," she replied.

"Well, I'll take a look around. Maybe you left it in a booth."

"Helen Meredith," I said when the bartender left. Here's to you!" We clicked our glasses together and drained them down. Helen choked a bit and followed her shot down with the short beer chaser.

"Ahhh," she sighed. "Harry, I'm going to tell you something while I'm still able to tell you. I haven't lived with my husband for more than ten years, and even though I don't wear a ring, I'm still married."

"You don't have to convince me."

"But I want to tell you. I live with my mother in San Sienna. Do you know where that is?"

"Sure. It's a couple of hundred miles down the coast. Noted for tourists, beaches, a mission and money. Nothing else."

"That's right. Well as I told you, I drink. In the past two years I've managed to embarrass Mother many times. It's a small community and we're both well-known so I decided the best thing to do was get out. This morning I was half-drunk, half-hungover, and I bought a bottle and I left. For good. But I hit the bottle so hard I'm not sure whether I came to San Francisco on the bus or on the train."

"I'm willing to lay odds of two to one it was the bus."

"You're probably right. I really don't remember."

The bartender brought us our second drink. He shook his

head emphatically. "You didn't leave no purse in here, miss. You might've thought you did, but you didn't."

"Thanks for looking," I told him. "After we finish this one," I said to Helen, "we'll go back down to the bus station and I'll find your purse for you. Then you'd better head back for San Sienna and Mother."

Helen shook her head back and forth slowly. "No. I'm not going back. Never."

"That's your business. Not mine."

We finished our second drink and left the bar. It was a long walk to the bus station. Market Street blocks are long and crowded. Helen hung on to my arm possesively, and by the time we reached the station she had sobered considerably. The place was jampacked with servicemen of all kinds and a liberal sprinkling of civilians. The Greyhound station is the jumping-off place for servicemen. San Francisco is the hub for all the spokes leading to air bases, navy bases and army posts that dot the bay area.

"Does the bus station look familiar to you?"

"Of course!" She laughed. "I've been to San Francisco many times. I always come up on the bus for my Christmas shopping."

I felt a little foolish. "Let's start looking then." She handed me the numbered key. There are a lot of parcel lockers inside the Greyhound station and many more out on the waiting ramp, but in a few minutes we were able to locate the locker. It was in the first row to the left of the Ladies' Room. I inserted the key and opened the locker.

I took the suitcase out of the locker and handed it to Helen. She unsnapped the two catches on the aluminum over-nighter and raised the lid. Her tiny hands ruffled deftly through the clothing. There wasn't any purse. I looked. No purse. I felt around inside the locker.

No purse.

"Do you suppose I could have left it in some other bar, Harry?" She asked me worriedly. "Somewhere between here and the cafe?"

"That's probably what you did, all right. And if you did, you can kiss it goodbye. How much money did you have?"

"I don't know, but drunk or sober I wouldn't have left San Sienna broke. I know I had some traveler's checks."

I took my money out of my watch pocket. There were eight dollars and seventy cents. I gave the five dollar bill to Helen. "This five'll get you a ticket back to San Sienna. You'd better get one."

Helen shook her head vigorously this time and firmly set her mouth. "I'm not going back, Harry. I told you I wasn't and I meant it." She held the bill out to me. "Take it back; I don't want it."

"No, you go ahead and keep it. We'll consider it a loan. But I'm going to take you to a hotel. If I turned you loose you'd drink it up."

"It didn't take you long to get to know me, did it?" She giggled.

"I don't know you. It's just that I know what I'd do. Come on, we'll find a hotel."

I picked up the light suitcase and we left the station. We crossed Market Street and at Powell we turned and entered the first hotel that looked satisfactory to me. There are more than a dozen hotels on Powell Street, all of them adequate, and it was our best bet to find a vacancy. The hotel we entered was furnished in cheap modern furniture and the floor was covered with a rose wall-to-wall carpet. There were several green plants scattered about, all of them set in white pots with wrought-iron legs, and by each foam-cushioned lobby chair there were skinny, black wrought-iron ash-stands. We crossed the empty lobby to the desk and I set the bag on the floor. The desk clerk was a fairly young man with sleek black hair. He looked up from his comic book with surly gray eyes.

"Sorry," he said flatly. "No doubles left. Just singles."

"That's fine," I said. "That's what I want."

Helen signed the register card. Her handwriting was cramped and it slanted to the left, almost microscopic in size. She put the pen back into the holder and folded her arms across her chest.

"The lady will pay in advance," I said to the clerk, without looking at Helen. She frowned fiercely for a second then in spite of herself, she giggled and gave the clerk the five dollar bill. He gave her two ones in return. The night clerk also doubled as a bell boy and he came out from behind the desk with Helen's key in his hand.

"You want to go up now?" he asked Helen, pointedly ignoring me.

"I've still got two dollars," Helen said to me. "I'll buy you a drink!"

"No. You go to bed. You've had enough for one day."

"I'll buy you one tomorrow then."

"Tomorrow will be time enough," I said.

Helen's eyes were glassy and her eyelids were heavy. It was difficult for her to hold them open. In the warmth of the lobby she was beginning to stagger a little bit. The night clerk opened the door to the self-operated elevator and helped her in holding her by the arm. I selected a comfortable chair near the desk and waited in the lobby until he returned. He didn't like it when he saw me sitting there.

"Do you think she'll manage all right?" I asked him.

"She managed to lock the door after I left," he replied dryly.

"Fine. Good night."

I left the hotel and walked up Powell as far as Lefty's, ordered a drink at the bar. It was dull, drinking alone, after drinking with Helen. She was the most attractive woman I had met in years. There was a quality about her that appealed to me. The fact that she was an alcoholic didn't make any difference to me. In a way, I was an alcoholic myself. She wasn't afraid to admit that she was a drunk; she was well aware of it, and she didn't have any intention to stop drinking. It wasn't necessary for her to tell me she was a drunk. I can spot an alcoholic in two minutes. Helen was still a good-looking woman, and she'd been drinking for a long time. I never expected to see her again. If I wanted to, I suppose it would have been easy enough. All I had to do was go down to her hotel in the morning, and . . .

I finished my drink quickly and left the bar. I didn't feel like drinking any more. I crossed the street and waited for my cable car. In a few minutes it dragged up the hill, slowed down at the corner, and I jumped on. I gave the conductor my fare and went inside where it was warmer. Usually, I sat in the outside section where I could smoke, but I was cold that night, my entire body was chilled.

On the long ride home I decided it would be best to steer clear of a woman like Helen.

finders keepers   2

I got out of bed the next morning at ten, and still half-asleep, put the coffee pot on the two-ring gas burner. I padded next door to the bathroom, stood under the hot water of the shower for fifteen minutes, shaved, and returned to my room. It was the last one on the left, downstairs in Mrs. Frances McQuade's roominghouse. The house was on a fairly quiet street and my room was well separated from the other rooms and roomers. This enabled me to drink in my room without bothering anybody, and nobody could bother me.

I sat down at the table, poured a cup of black coffee and let my mind think about Helen. I tried to define what there was about her that attracted me. Class. That was it. I didn't intend to do anything about the way I felt, but it was pleasant to let my mind explore the possibilities. I finished my coffee and looked around the room. Not only was it an ugly room; it was a filthy room. The walls were covered with a dull gray paper spotted with small crimson flowers. There was a sink in one corner, and next to it the gas burner in a small alcove. My bed was a double, and the head and foot-boards were made of brass rods ornately twisted and tortured into circular designs. The dresser was metal, painted to look like maple or walnut, some kind of wood, and each leg rested in a small can of water. I kept my food in the bottom drawer and the cans of water kept the ants away. There were no pictures on the walls and no rug upon the floor, just a square piece of tangerine linoleum under the sink.

The room was in foul shape. Dirty shirts and dirty socks were scattered around, the dresser was messy with newspapers, book matches, my set of oil paints; and the floor was covered with gently moving dust motes. Lined up beneath the sink were seven empty gin bottles and an overflowing paper sack full of empty beer cans. The window was dirty and the sleazy cotton curtains were dusty. Dust was on everything . . .

Suppose, by some chance, I had brought Helen home with me the night before? I sadly shook my head. Here was a project for me; I'd clean my room. A momentous decision.

I slipped into my shoes and blue gabardine slacks and walked down the hall to Mrs. McQuade's room.

"Good morning," I said, when she opened the door. "I want to borrow your broom and mop."

"The broom and mop are in the closet," she said, and closed the door again.

Mrs. McQuade had a few eccentricities, but she was a kind, motherly type of woman. Her hair was always freshly blued and whenever I thought about it I would comment on how nice it looked. Why women with beautiful white hair doctor it with bluing has always been a mystery to me.

I found the broom and a rag mop and returned to my room.

I spent the rest of the morning cleaning the room, even going so far as to wash my window inside and out. The curtains needed washing but I shook the dust out of them and hung them back on the rod. Dusted and cleaned, the room looked fairly presentable, even with its ancient, battered furniture. I was dirty again so I took another shower before I dressed. I put my bundle of laundry under my arm, dragged the mop and broom behind me, and leaned them up against Mrs. McQuade's door.

I left the house and dumped my dirty laundry off at the Spotless Cleaner on my way to the corner and Big Mike's Bar and Grill. This was my real home, Big Mike's, and I spent more time in this bar than anywhere else. It was a friendly place, old-fashioned, with sawdust on the floor, and the walls paneled in dark oak. The bar was long and narrow, extending the length of the room, and it had a section with cushioned stools and another section with a rail for those who preferred to stand. There were a few booths along the wall, but there was also a dining-room next door that could be entered either from the street outside or from the barroom. The food was good, reasonable, and there was plenty of it. I seldom ate anything at Mike's. Food costs money and money spent for food is money wasted. When I got hungry, which was seldom, I ate at Benny's.

I took my regular seat at the end of the bar and ordered a draught beer. It was lunch hour and very busy, but both of the bartenders knew me well and when my stein was emptied one of them would quickly fill it again. After one-thirty, the bar was clear of the lunch crowd and Big Mike joined me in a beer.

"You're a little late today, Harry," Mike said jokingly. He had a deep pleasant voice.

"Couldn't be helped."

Mike was an enormous man; everything about him was large, especially his head and hands. The habitual white shirt and full-sized apron he wore added to his look of massiveness. His face was badly scarred, but it didn't make him look hard or tough; it gave him a kindly, mellowed expression. He could be tough when it was necessary, however, and he was his own bouncer. The bar and grill belonged to him alone, and it had been purchased by his savings after ten years of professional football—all of it on the line, as a right tackle.

"How does my tab stand these days, Mike?" I asked him.

"I'll check." He looked in the credit book hanging by a string next to the cash register. "Not too bad," he smiled. "Twelve twenty-five. Worried about it?"

"When it gets to fifteen, cut me off, will you, Mike?"

"If I do you'll give me an argument."

"Don't pay any attention to me. Cut me off just the same."

"Okay." He shrugged his heavy shoulders. "We've gone through this before, we might as well go through it again."

"I'm not that bad, Mike."

"I honestly believe you don't know how bad you really are when you're loaded." He laughed to show he was joking, finished his beer, and lumbered back to the kitchen. I drank several beers, nursing them along, and at two thirty I left the bar to go to work.

We picked up a little business from the theatre crowd when the afternoon show at the Bijou got out at three-thirty, and after that the cafe was fairly quiet until five. When things were busy, there was too much work for only one counterman, and I met myself coming and going. Benny was of no help at all. He never stirred all day from his seat behind the register. I don't know how he had the patience to sit like that from seven in the morning until eleven at night. His only enjoyment in life was obtained by eating orange gum-drops and counting his money at night. Once that day, during a lull, when no one was in the cafe, he tried to kid me about Helen. I didn't like it.

"Come on, Harry, where'd you take her last night?"

"Just forget about it, Benny. There's nothing to tell." I went in to the kitchen to get away from him. I don't like that kind of talk. It's dirty. All of a sudden, all ten seats at the counter were filled, and I was too busy to think of anything except what I was doing. In addition to taking the orders, I had to prepare the food and serve it myself. It was quite a job to handle alone, even though Benny didn't run a regular lunch or dinner menu. Just when things are running well and the orders are simple things like sandwiches, bowls of chile, and coffee, a damned aesthete will come in and order soft-boiled eggs wanting them two-and-one-half minutes in the water or something like that. But I like to work and the busier I am the better I like it. When I'm busy I don't have time to think about when I'll get my next drink.

Ten o'clock rolled around at last, the hour I liked the best of all. The traffic was always thin about this time and I only had another hour to go before I could have a drink. I felt a little hungry—I hadn't eaten anything all day—and I made myself a bacon and tomato sandwich. I walked around the counter and sat down to eat it. Benny eyed my sandwich hungrily.

"How about fixing me one of those, Harry?" he asked.

"Sure. Soon as I finish."

"Fix me one too," a feminine voice said lightly. I glanced to the left and there was Helen, standing in the doorway.

"You came back." My voice sounded flat and strained. No longer interested in food, I pushed my sandwich away from me.

"I told you I would. I owe you a drink. Remember?" She had a black patent leather purse in her hand. "See?" She shook the purse in the air. "I found it."

"Do you really want a sandwich?" I asked her, getting to my feet.

"No." She shook her head. "I was just talking."

"Wait right there," I said firmly, pointing my finger at Helen. "I'll be back in one second."

I went into the back room, and feverishly removed the dirty white jacket and leather tie. I changed into my own tie and sport jacket. Benny was ringing up thirty-one cents on the register when I came back. Helen had paid him for the coffee she had drunk the night before. Trust Benny to get his money.

I took Helen's arm, and Benny looked at us both with some surprise.

"Now just where in the hell do you think you're going?" he asked acidly.

"I quit. Come on, Helen." We walked through the open door.

"Hey!" He shouted after us, and I know that he said something else, but by that time we were walking down the street and well out of range.

first night $\boxed{3}$

"**D**id you really quit just like that?" Helen asked me as we walked down the street. Her voice was more amused than incredulous.

"Sure. You said you were going to buy me a drink. That's much more important than working."

"Here we are then." Helen pointed to the entrance door of the bar where we'd had our drinks the night before. "Is this all right?"

I smiled. "It's the nearest." We went inside and sat down at the bar. The bartender recognized Helen right away. He nodded pleasantly to me and then asked Helen: "Find your purse all right?"

"Sure did," Helen said happily.

"Now I'm glad to hear that," the bartender said. "I was

afraid somebody might have picked it up and gone south with it. You know how these things happen sometimes. What'll you have?"

"Double gin and tonic for me," I said.

"Don't change it," Helen ordered, stringing along.

As soon as the bartender left to fix our drinks I took a sideways look at Helen. She wasn't tight, not even mellow, but barely under the influence; just enough under to give her a warm, rosy-cheeked color.

"Where did you find your purse, by the way?" I asked Helen.

"It was easy," she laughed merrily. "But I didn't think so this morning." She opened her purse, put enough change down on the bar to pay for the check and handed me a five dollar bill. "Now we're even, Harry."

"Thanks," I said folding the bill and shoving it into my watch pocket, "I can use it."

"This morning," she began slowly, "I woke up in that miserable little hotel room with a hangover to end them all. God, I felt rotten! I could remember everything pretty well—you going down to the bus station with me, getting the room and so on, but the rest of the day was·nothing. Did you ever get like that?"

"I recall a similar experience," I admitted.

"All I had was two dollars, as you know, so after I showered and dressed I checked out of the hotel, leaving my bag at the desk. I was hungry, so I ate breakfast and had four cups of coffee, black, and tried to figure out what to do next.

"Without money, I was in a bad way—" She quickly finished her drink and shook the ice in her glass at the bartender for another. I downed mine fast in order to join her for the next round.

"So I returned to the bus station after breakfast and started from there." She smiled slyly and sipped her drink. "Now where would you have looked for the purse, Harry?"

I thought the question over for a moment. "The nearest bar?"

"Correct!" She laughed appreciatively. "That's where I found it. The first bar to the left of the station. There was a different bartender on duty—about eleven this morning—and he didn't know me, of course, but I described my bag and it was there, under the shelf by the cash register. At first he wouldn't give it to me because there wasn't any identification inside. Like a driver's license, something like that, but my traveler's checks were in the bag and after I wrote my name on a piece of paper and he compared the signatures on the checks he gave it to me. The first thing I did was cash a check and buy him a drink, joining him, of course."

"No money at all?"

"Just the traveler's checks. I'm satisfied. Two hundred dollars in traveler's checks is better than money."

"Cash a couple then and let's get out of here," I said happily. "This isn't the only bar in San Francisco."

We went to several places that night and knowing where to go is a mighty tricky business. Having lived in San Francisco for more than a year I could just about tell and I was very careful about the places I took her to. I didn't want to embarrass Helen any—not that she would have given a damn—but I wanted to have a good time, and I wanted her to have a good time too.

The last night club we were in was The Dolphin. I had been there once before, when I was in the chips, and I knew Helen would like it. It's a club you have to know about or you can't find it. It's down an alley off Divisadero Street and I had to explain to the taxicab driver how to get there. There isn't any lettered sign over the door; just a large, blue neon fish blinking intermittently, and the fish itself doesn't look like a dolphin. But once inside you know you're in The Dolphin, because the name is in blue letters on the menu, and the prices won't let you forget where you are. We entered and luckily found a booth well away from the bar. The club is designed with a South Seas effect, and the drinks are served in tall, thick glasses, the size and shape of a vase. The booth we sat in was very soft, padded thickly with foam rubber, and both of us had had enough to drink to appreciate the atmosphere and the deep, gloomy lighting that made it almost impossible to see across the room. The waiter appeared at our table out of the darkness and handed each of us a menu. He was a Mexican, naked except for a grass skirt, and made up to look like an islander of some sort: there were blue and yellow streaks of paint on his brown face, and he wore a shark's-teeth necklace.

"Do you still have the Dolphin Special?" I asked him.

"Certainly," he said politely. "And something to eat? Poi, dried squid, bird's-nest soup, breadfruit au gratin, sago palm salad—"

Helen's laugh startled the waiter. "No thanks," she said. "I guess I'm not hungry."

"Just bring us two of the Dolphin Specials," I told him. He nodded solemnly and left for the bar. The Special is a good drink; it contains five varieties of rum, mint, plenty of snow-ice, and it's decorated with orange slices, pineapple slices and cherries with a sprinkling of sugar cane gratings floating on top. I needed at least two of them. I had to build up my nerve.

After the waiter brought our drinks I lighted cigarettes and we smoked silently, dumping the ashes into the large abalone shell on the table that served as an ash-tray. The trio hummed into action and the music floating our way gave me a wistful feeling of nostalgia. The trio consisted of chimes, theremin and electric guitar and the unusual quality of the theremin prevented me from recognizing the melody of the song although I was certain I knew what it was.

With sudden impulsive boldness I put my hand on Helen's knee. Her knee jumped under the touch of my hand, quivered and was still again. She didn't knock my hand away. I drank my drink, outwardly calm, bringing my glass up to my lips with my free hand, and wondering vaguely what to do next.

"Helen," I said, my voice a little hoarse, "I've been hoping and dreading to see you all day. I didn't really expect to see you, and yet, when I thought I wouldn't, my heart would sort of knot up."

"Why, Harry, you're a poet!"

"No, I'm serious. I'm trying to tell you how I feel about you."

"I didn't mean to be rude or flippant, Harry. I feel very close to you, and trying to talk about it isn't any good."

"I've had terrible luck with women, Helen," I said, "and for the last two years I've kept away from them. I didn't want to go through it all again—you know, the bickering, the jealousy, nagging, that sort of thing. Am I scaring you off?"

"You couldn't if you tried, Harry. You're my kind of man and it isn't hard to say so. What I mean is—you're somebody, underneath, a person, and not just another man. See?" She shook her head impatiently. "I told you I couldn't talk about it."

"One thing I want to get straight is this," I said. "I'll never tell you that I love you."

"That word doesn't mean anything anyway."

"I never thought I'd hear a woman say that. But it's the truth. Love is in what you do, not in what you say. Couples work themselves into a hypnotic state daily by repeating to each other over and over again that they love each other. And they don't know the meaning of the word. They also say they love a certain brand of tooth paste and a certain brand of cereal in the same tone of voice."

Cautiously, I gathered the material of her skirt with my fingers until the hem was above her knee. My hand squeezed the warm flesh above her stocking. It was soft as only a woman's thigh is soft. She spread her legs at the touch of my hand and calmly sipped her drink. I tried to go a little higher and she clamped her legs on my hand.

"After all, Harry," she chided me, "we're not alone, you know."

I took my hand away from the softness of her thigh and she pulled her skirt down, smiling at me sympathetically. With trembling hands I lighted a cigarette. I didn't know what to do or what to say next. I felt as immature and inept as a teen-ager on his first date. And Helen wasn't helping me at all. I couldn't imagine what she was thinking about my crude and foolish passes.

"Helen," I blurted out like a schoolboy, "will you sleep with me tonight?" I felt like I had staked my life on the turn of a card.

"Why, Harry! What a thing to say." Her eyes didn't twinkle, that is impossible, but they came close to it. Very close. "Where else did you think I was going if I didn't go home with you?"

"I don't know," I said honestly.

"You didn't have to ask me like that. I thought there was an understanding between us, that it was understood."

"I don't like to take people for granted."

"In that case then, I'll tell you. I'm going home with you."

"I hope we're compatible," I said. "Then everything will be perfect."

"We are. I know it."

"I'm pretty much of a failure in life, Helen. Does it matter to you?"

"No. Nothing matters to me." Her voice had a resigned quality and yet it was quietly confident. There was a tragic look in her brown eyes, but her mouth was smiling. It was the smile of a little girl who knows a secret and isn't going to tell it. I held her hand in mine. It was a tiny, almost pudgy band, soft and warm and trusting. We finished our drinks.

"Do you want another?" I asked her.

"Not really. After I go to the potty I want you to take me home." I helped her out of the booth. It wasn't easy for her to hold her feet, and she had had more to drink than I'd had. I watched her affectionately as she picked her way across the dimly lighted room. She was everything I ever wanted in a woman.

When she returned to the table I took the twenty she gave me and paid for the drinks. We walked to the mouth of the alley and I hailed a taxi. I gave my address to the driver and we settled back on the seat. I took Helen in my arms and kissed her.

"It makes me dizzy," she said. "Roll the windows down."

I had to laugh, but I rolled the windows down. The night air was cold and it was a long ride to my neighborhood. By the time we reached the roominghouse I knew she would be all right. I lit two cigarettes, passed one to Helen. She took one deep drag, tossed it out the window.

"I'm a little nervous, Harry."

"Why?"

"It's been a long time. Years, in fact."

"It doesn't change."

"Please don't say that! Be gentle with me, Harry."

"How could I be otherwise? You're just a little girl."

"I trust you, Harry."

The taxi pulled up in front of my roominghouse and we got out. We climbed the stairs quietly and walked down the long, dark hall to my room. There was only a single 40-watt bulb above the bathroom door to light the entire length of the hall. I unlocked my door and guided Helen inside. It took me a while to find the dangling string to the overhead light in the ceiling. Finding it at last, I flooded the room with light. I pulled the shade down and Helen looked the shabby room over with an amused smile.

"You're a good housekeeper," she said.

"Today anyway. I must have expected company," I said nervously.

Slowly, we started to undress. The more clothes we took off, the slower we got.

"Hadn't you better turn the light off?" Helen asked, timidly.

"No," I said firmly, "I don't want it that way."

We didn't hesitate any longer. Both of us undressed hurriedly. Helen crawled to the center of the bed, rolled over on her back and put her hands behind her head. She kept her eyes on the ceiling. Her breasts were small and the slenderness of her hips made her legs look longer than they were. Her skin was pale, almost like living mother-of-pearl, except for the flush that lay on her face like a delicately tinted rose. I stood in the center of the room and I could have watched her forever. I pulled the light cord and got into bed.

At first I just held her hot body against mine, she was trembling so hard. I covered her face with soft little kisses, her throat, her breasts. When my lips touched the tiny nipples of her breasts she sighed and relaxed somewhat. Her body still trembled, but it wasn't from fear. As soon as the nipples hardened I kissed her roughly on the mouth and she whimpered, dug her fingernails into my shoulders. She bit my lower lip with her sharp little teeth and I felt the blood spurt into my mouth.

"Now, Harry! Now!" She murmured softly.

It was even better than I'd thought it would be.

nude model **4**

When I awoke the next morning Helen was curled up beside me. Her face was flushed with sleep and her nice hair curled all over her head. If it hadn't been for the single strand of pure silver hair she wouldn't have looked more than thirteen years old. I kissed her on the mouth and she opened her eyes. She sat up and stretched luxuriously, immediately awake, like a cat.

"I've never slept better in my entire life," she said.

"I'll fix some coffee. Then while you're in the bathroom, I'd better go down the hall and tell Mrs. McQuade you're here."

"Who is she?"

"The landlady. You'll meet her later on."

"Oh. What're you going to tell her?"

"I'll tell her we're married. We had a long, trial separation and now we've decided to try it again. It's a pretty thin story, but it'll hold."

"I feel married to you, Harry."

"For all practical purposes, we are married."

I got out of bed, crossed to the dresser, and tossed a clean, white shirt to Helen. She put it on and the shirt tail came to her knees. After she rolled up the sleeves she left the room. I put on my slacks and a T-shirt, fixed the coffee and lighted the gas burner under it, walked down the hall and knocked on Mrs. McQuade's door.

"Good morning, Mrs. McQuade," I said, when she opened the door.

"You're not going to clean your room again?" she asked with mock surprise in her voice.

"No." I laughed. "Two days in a row would be overdoing it. I just wanted to tell you my wife was back."

"I didn't even know you were married!" She raised her eyebrows.

"Oh, yes! I've been married a good many years. We were separated, but we've decided to try it again. I'll bring Helen down after a while. I want you to meet her."

"I'm very happy for you, Mr. Jordan."

"I think it'll work this time."

"Would you like a larger room?" she asked eagerly. "The front upstairs room is vacant, and if you want me to—"

"No, thanks," I said quickly, "we'll be all right where we are."

I knew Mrs. McQuade didn't believe me, but a woman running a roominghouse doesn't get surprised at anything. She didn't mention it right then, but by the end of the week I could expect an increase in rent. That is the way those things go.

The coffee was ready and when Helen returned I finished my cup quickly and poured one for her.

"We've only got one cup," I said apologetically.

"We'll have to get another one."

After I shaved, and both of us were dressed, we finished the pot of coffee, taking turns with the cup. Helen borrowed my comb, painted her dark lipstick on with a tiny brush, and she was ready for the street.

"Don't you even use powder?" I asked her curiously.

"Uh uh. Just lipstick."

"We'd better go down and get your suitcase."

"I'm ready."

Mrs. McQuade and Miss Foxhall, a retired schoolteacher, were standing by the front door when we came down the hall. Mrs. McQuade had a broom in her hand, and Miss Foxhall held an armful of books; she was either going to or returning from the neighborhood branch public library. They both eyed Helen curiously, Mrs. McQuade with a smile, Miss Foxhall with hostility. I introduced Helen to the two older women. Mrs. McQuade wiped her hands on her apron and shook Helen's hand. Miss Foxhall snorted audibly, pushed roughly between us and hurried up the stairs without a word. I noticed that the top book in the stack she carried was *Ivanhoe*, by Sir Walter Scott.

"You're a very pretty girl, Mrs. Jordan," Mrs. McQuade said sincerely. All three of us pretended to ignore the rudeness of Miss Foxhall.

We walked down the block to Big Mike's, Helen holding my arm. The sun was shining and despite a slight persisting hangover I was a proud and happy man. Everyone who passed stared at Helen, and to know that she was mine made me straighten my back and hold my head erect. We entered Mike's and sat down at the bar. Big Mike joined us at once.

"You're on time today, Harry." He similed.

"Mike, I want you to meet my wife. Helen Jordan, Big Mike."

"How do you do, Mrs. Jordan? This calls for one on the house. Now what'll it be?"

"Since it's on the house, Mike," Helen smiled, "I'll have a double bourbon and water."

"Double gin and tonic for me," I added.

Mike set up our drinks, drew a short beer for himself, and we raised our glasses in salute. He returned to his work table where he was slicing oranges, sticking toothpicks into cherries, and preparing generally for the noon-hour rush period. It was quite early to be drinking and Helen and I were the only people sitting at the bar. Rodney, the crippled newsboy, was eating breakfast in one of the booths along the wall. He waved to me with his fork and I winked at him.

After we finished our drinks we caught the cable car to the hotel on Powell Street and picked up Helen's suitcase. It only took a minute and we were able to catch the same car back, after it was ready to climb the hill again and turned on the Market Street turnaround. The round trip took more than an hour.

"I'm disgustingly sober," Helen said, as we stood on the curb, waiting for the light to change.

"What do you want to do? I'll give you two choices. We can drink in Big Mike's or we can get a bottle and go back to the room."

"Let's get a bottle, by all means."

At Mr. Watson's delicatessen I bought a fifth of gin, a fifth of whiskey and a cardboard carrier of six small bottles of soda. To nibble on, in case we happened to get hungry, I added a box of cheese crackers to the stack. We returned to our room and I removed my jacket and shirt. Helen took off her suit and hung it carefully in the closet. While I fixed the drinks Helen explored the room, digging into everything. She pulled out all of the dresser drawers, then examined the accumulation of junk above the sink. It was pleasant to watch her walking around the room in her slip. She discovered my box of oil paints on the shelf, brought it to the table and opened it.

"Do you paint, Harry?"

"At one time I did. That's the first time that box has been opened in three years." I handed her a drink. "There isn't any ice."

"All ice does is take up room. Why don't you paint any more?"

I looked into the opened paint box. The caps were tightly screwed on all of the tubes and most of the colors were there, all except yellow ochre and zinc white. I fingered the brushes, ran a finger over the edges of the bristles. They were in good shape, still usable, and there was a full package of charcoal sticks.

"I discovered I couldn't paint, that's why. It took me a long time to accept it, but after I found out I gave it up."

"Who told you you couldn't paint?"

"Did you ever do any painting?"

"Some. I graduated from Mills College, where they taught us something about everything. I even learned how to shoot a bow and arrow."

"I'll tell you how it is about painting, Helen, the way it was with me. It was a love affair. I used painting as a substitute for love. All painters do; it's their nature. When you're painting, the pain in your stomach drives you on to a climax of pure feeling, and if you're any good the feeling is transmitted to the canvas. In color, in form, in line and they blend together in a perfect design that delights your eye and makes your heart beat a little faster. That's what painting meant to me, and then it turned in to an unsuccessful love affair, and we broke it off. I'm over it now, as much as I'll ever be, and certainly the world of art hasn't suffered."

"Who told you to give it up? Some critic?"

"Nobody had to tell me. I found it out for myself, the hard way. Before the war I went to the Art Institute in Chicago for two years, and after the war I took advantage of the GI Bill and studied another year in Los Angeles."

"Wouldn't anybody buy your work? Was that it?"

"No, that isn't it. I never could finish anything I started. I'd get an idea, block it out, start on it, and then when I'd get about halfway through I'd discover the idea was terrible. And I couldn't finish a picture when I knew it wasn't going to be any good. I taught for a while, but that wasn't any good either."

Helen wasn't looking at me. She had walked to the window and appeared to be studying the littered backyard next door with great interest. I knew exactly what she had on her mind. The Great American Tradition: *You* can do anything you think you can do! All Americans believe in it. What a joke that is! Can a jockey last ten rounds with Rocky Marciano? Can Marciano ride in the Kentucky Derby? Can a poet make his living by writing poetry? The entire premise was so false it was stupid to contemplate. Helen finished her drink, turned around, and set the empty glass on the table.

"Harry," she said seriously, "I want you to do something for me."

"I'll do anything for you."

"No, not just like that. I want you to hear what it is first."

"It sounds serious."

"It is. I want you to paint my portrait."

"I don't think I could do it." I shrugged, looked into my empty glass. "It's been more than three years since I tried to paint anything, and portraits are hard. To do a good one, anyway, and if I were to paint you, I'd want it to be perfect. It would have to be, and I'm not capable of it."

"I want you to paint it anyway."

"How about a sketch? If you want a picture of yourself, I can draw a charcoal likeness in five minutes."

"No. I want you to paint an honest-to-God oil painting of me."

"You really want me to; this isn't just a whim?"

"I really want you to." Her face was as deadly serious as her voice.

I thought it over and it made me feel a little sick to my stomach. The mere thought of painting again made me tremble. It was like asking a pilot to take an airplane up again after a bad crash; a crash that has left him horribly disfigured and frightened. Helen meant well. She wanted me to prove to myself that I was wrong . . . that I could do anything I really wanted to do. That is, as long as she was there to help me along by her inspiration and encouragement. More than anything else in the world, I wanted to please her.

"It takes time to paint a portrait," I said.

"We've got the time. We've got forever."

"Give me some money then."

"How much do you need?"

"I don't know. I'll need a canvas, an easel, linseed oil, turpentine, I don't know what all. I'll have to look around when I get to the art store."

"I'm going with you." She began to dress.

Once again, we made the long trip downtown by cable car. We went to an art store on Polk Street and I picked out a cheap metal easel, in addition to the regular supplies, and a large canvas, thirty by thirty-four inches. As long as I had decided to paint Helen's portrait, I was going to do it right. We left the store, both of us loaded down with bundles and I searched the streets for a taxi. Helen didn't want to return home immediately.

"You're doing something for me," she said, "and I want to do something for you. Before we go home I'm going to buy you a new pair of pants and a new sport coat."

"You can't do it, Helen," I protested. "We've spent too much already."

She had her way, but I didn't let her spend too much money on my new clothes. I insisted on buying a pair of gray corduroy trousers, and a dark blue corduroy jacket at the nearest Army and Navy surplus store. These were cheap clothes, but they satisfied Helen's desire to do something nice for me. I certainly needed them. Wearing my new clothes in the taxi, on the way home, and looking at all of the new art supplies piled on the floor, gave me a warm feeling inside and a pleasant tingling of anticipation.

The minute we entered our room I removed my new jacket and set up the easel. While I opened the paints and arranged the materials on a straight backed chair next to the easel, Helen fixed fresh drinks. She held up her glass and posed, a haughty expression on her face.

"Look, Harry. Woman of Distinction." We both laughed. "Do you want me to pose like this?"

The pose I wanted Helen to take wasn't difficult. The hard part was to paint her in the way I wanted to express my feelings for her. I wanted to capture the mother-of-pearl of her body, the secret of her smile, the strand of silver in her hair, the jet, arched brows, the tragedy in her brown, gold-flecked eyes. I wasn't capable of it; I knew that in advance. I placed two pillows on the floor, close to the bed, so she could lean back against the bed to support her back. The light from the window would fall across her body and create sharp and difficult shadows. The hard way, like always, I took the hard way.

"Take off your clothes, Helen, and sit down on the pillows."

After Helen had removed her clothes and settled herself comfortably I rearranged her arms, her right hand in her lap, her left arm stretched full length on the bed. Her legs were straight out, with the right ankle crossed over the other. The similarity between Helen and the woman in the *Olympia* almost took my breath away with the awesomeness of it.

"Is that comfortable?" I asked her.

"It feels all right. How long do you want me to stay like this?"

"Just remember it, that's all. When I tell you to pose, get into it, otherwise, sit anyway you like. As I told you, this is going to take a long time. Drink your drink, talk, or smile that smile of yours. Okay?"

"I'm ready."

I started with the charcoal, blocking in Helen's figure. She was sitting *too* stiffly, eyes straight ahead, tense. To me, the drawing is everything and I wanted her to talk, to get animation in her face.

"Talk to me, Helen," I told her.

"Is it all right?"

"Sure. I want you to talk. Tell me about Mills College. What did you major in?"

"Geology."

"That's a strange subject for a woman to take. What made you major in geology?"

"I was romantic in those days, Harry. I liked rocks and I thought geology was fascinating, but secretly, I thought if I could learn geology I could get away from Mother. I used to dream about going to Tibet or South America with some archeological expedition. Mother was never in the dream, but she was with me all the way through college. I had a miserable college education. She came with me and we took an apartment together. While the other girls lived in sororities and had a good time I studied. She stood right over me, just like she did all the way through high school. My grades were fine, the highest in my class. Not that I was a brilliant student, but because I didn't do anything except study.

"In the summers we went back to San Sienna. One summer we went to Honolulu, and once to Mexico City so I could look at ruins. The trips weren't any fun, because Mother was along. No night life, no dates, no romance."

"It sounds terrible."

"It was, believe me." She lapsed into silence, brooding.

It was a pleasant day. Helen made a drink for herself once in awhile, but I didn't join her; I was much too busy. The outline shaped well and I was satisfied with the progress I had made. By the time the light failed Helen had finished the bottle of whiskey and was more than a little tight. We were both extremely tired from the unaccustomed activity. Helen would find that modeling was one of the toughest professions in the world before we were through.

We dressed and walked down the street to Big Mike's for dinner. I ordered steaks from Tommy the waiter, and while we waited we sat at the end of the bar and had a drink. There were three workmen in overalls occupying the booth opposite from where we were sitting and their table was completely covered with beer cans. They made a few choice nasty remarks about Helen and me, but I ignored them. Big Mike was a friend of mine and I didn't want to cause any trouble in his bar.

"Look at that," the man wearing white overalls said. "Ain't that the limit?" His voice was loud, coarse, and it carried the length of the barroom.

"By God," the man on the inside said, "I believe I've seen it *all* now!" He nodded his head solemnly. "Yes, sir, I've

seen it *all!*" His voice had a forced quality of comic serious-
ness and his companions laughed.

Helen's face had changed from pale to chalky white. She
quickly finished her drink, set the glass on the bar and took
my arm. "Come on Harry," she said anxiously, "let's go
inside the dining room and find a table."

"All right." My voice sounded as though it belonged to
someone else.

We climbed down from the stools and crossed to the dining room entrance. We paused in the doorway and I
searched the room for a table. One of the men shouldered
us apart and stared insolently at Helen.

"Why don't you try me for size, baby?"

His two friends were standing behind me and they
snickered.

Without a word I viciously kicked the man in front of me
in the crotch. The insolent smile left his face in a hurry. His
puffy red face lost its color and he clutched his groin with
both hands and sank to his knees. I kicked him in the
mouth and blood bubbled out of his ripped cheek from the
corner of his torn mouth all the way to his ear. I whirled
around quickly, expecting an attack from the two men
behind me, but Big Mike was holding both of them by the
collar. There was a wide grin on his multi-scarred face.

"Go ahead, Harry," he said gruffly, "finish the job. These
lice won't interfere."

The man was on his feet again; some of the color was
back in his mutilated face. He snatched a bread knife from
the waiter's work table and backed slowly across the room.

Many of the diners had left their tables and were crowded
against the far wall near the kitchen. I advanced on the man
cautiously, my arm widely spread. He lunged forward in a
desperate attempt to disembowel me, bringing the knife up
fast, aiming for my stomach. At the last moment I twisted
sideways and brought my right fist up from below my knee.
His jaw was wide open and my blow caught him flush below
the chin. He fell forward on the floor, like a slugged ox.

My entire body was shaking with fear and excitement. I
looked wildly around the room for Helen. She was standing, back to the wall, frozen with fear. She ran to my side,
hugged me around the waist.

"Come on, Harry" She said tearfully. "Let's get out of here!"

"Nothing doing," I said stubbornly. "We ordered steaks and we're going to eat them."

I guided Helen to an empty table against the wall. Big Mike had bounced the other two workmen out and now he was back in the dining-room. Two waiters, at his nod, dragged the unconscious man out of the room through the kitchen exit. Mike came over to our table.

"I saw the whole thing, Harry," Tommy said "and if it goes to court or anything like that, I'll swear that he started the fight by pulling a knife on you!" He was so sincere I found it difficult to keep from laughing.

"Thanks, Tommy," I told him, "but I think that's the end of it."

I couldn't eat my steak and neither could Helen although both of us made a valiant try.

"The hell with it, Harry," Helen smiled. "Let's get a bottle and go home."

We left the grill, bought another fifth of whiskey at the delicatessen and returned to our room. My bottle of gin was scarcely tapped. I held it up to my lips, and drinking in short swallows, I drank until I almost passed out.

Helen had to undress me and put me to bed.

celebration 5

If there was anything I didn't want to do the next morning, it was paint. My head was vibrating like a struck gong and my stomach was full of fluttering, little winged creatures. Every muscle of my body ached and all I wanted to do was stay in bed and quietly nurse my hangover.

Helen was one of those rare persons who seldom get a hangover. She felt fine. She showered, dressed, left the house and returned with a fifth of whiskey and a paper sack filled with cold bottles of beer.

"Drink this beer," she ordered, "and let's get started. You

can't let a little thing like a fight and a hangover stop you."
She handed me an opened bottle of beer. I sat up in bed,
groaning, and let the icy beer flow down my throat. It
tasted marvelous, tangy, refreshing, and I could feel its
coldness all the way down. I drank some coffee, two more
beers and started to work.

I had to draw slowly at first. There was still a slight
tremor in my fingers, caused partly by the hangover, but
the unexpected fight the night before had a lot to do with it.
I've never been a fighter and when I thought about my
vicious assault on the man in Mike's, I could hardly believe
it had happened. Within a short time, Helen's beauty
pushed the ugly memory out of my head and I was more
interested in the development of her picture.

Painting or drawing from a nude model had never been
an exciting experience before, but Helen was something
else . . . I didn't have the feeling of detachment an artist is
supposed to have toward his model. I was definitely aware
of Helen's body as an instrument of love, and as my hangover gradually disappeared I couldn't work any longer
unless I did something about it . . .

Helen talked about the dullness of San Sienna as I
worked and from time to time she would take a shot from
the bottle of whiskey resting on the floor, following it down
with a sip of water. As she began to feel the drinks her voice
became animated. And so did I. Unable to stand it any
longer I tossed my charcoal stick down, scooped Helen
from the floor and dropped her sideways on the bed. She
laughed softly.

"It's about time," she said.

I dropped to my knees beside the bed, pressed my face
into her warm, soft belly and kissed her navel. She clutched
my hair with both hands and shoved my head down hard.

"Oh, yes, Harry! Make love to me! Make love to me . . ."

And I did. She didn't have to coax me.

It took all of the will power I could muster to work on the
picture again, but I managed, and surprisingly enough it
was much easier than it had been. With my body relaxed I
could now approach my work with the proper, necessary
detachment an artist must have if he is to get anywhere.
The drawing was beginning to look very well, and by four

in the afternoon when I couldn't stick it out any longer and quit for the day, I was exhilarated by my efforts and Helen was pleasantly tight from the whiskey.

After we were dressed I took a last look at the picture before leaving for Mike's.

"This is my first portrait," I told Helen as I opened the door for her. "And probably my last."

"I didn't know that, Harry," she said, somewhat surprised. "What kind of painting did you do? Landscapes?"

"No," I laughed. "Non-objective, or as you understand it, abstract."

"You mean these weird things with the lines going every which way, and the limp watches and stuff—"

"That's close enough." I couldn't explain what is impossible to explain. We went to Big Mike's, had dinner, and drank at the bar until closing time.

This was the pattern of our days for the next week and a half, except for one thing: I quit drinking. Not completely; I still drank beer, but I laid off whiskey and gin completely. I didn't need it any more. Painting and love were all I needed to make me happy. Helen continued to drink, and during the day, whether drunk or sober, if I told her to pose she assumed it without any trouble, and held it until I told her to relax.

For me, this was a fairly happy period. I hadn't realized how much I had missed painting. And with Helen for a model it was pure enjoyment. I seldom said anything. I was contented to merely paint and look at Helen. Often there were long silences between us when all we did was look at each other. These long periods usually ended up in bed without a word being spoken. It was as though our bodies had their own methods of communication. More relaxed, more sure of myself, I would take up my brush again and Helen would sit very much at ease, on the two pillows beside the bed and assume the pose I had given her. My Helen! *My Olympia!*

When I finished the drawing in charcoal I made a complete underpainting in tints and shades of burnt sienna, lightening the browns carefully with white and turpentine. The underpainting always makes me nervous. The all-important drawing which takes so many tedious hours is destroyed with the first stroke of the brush and replaced with shades of brown oil paint. The completed drawing, which is a picture worthy of framing by itself, is now a memory as the turpentine and oil soaks up the charcoal and replaces it with a tone in a different medium. But it is a base that will last through the years when the colors are applied over it. I had Helen look at the completed brown-tone painting.

"It looks wonderful, Harry! Is my figure that perfect?"

"It's the way it looks to me. Don't worry about your face. It's just drawn in a general way . . . the effects of the shadows."

"I'm not worried. It looks like me already."

"When I'm finished, it will be you," I said determinedly.

I started with the colors, boldly but slowly, in my old style. I didn't pay any attention to background, but concentrated on Helen's figure. At the time I felt that I shouldn't neglect the background, but no ideas came to me and I let it go. The painting was turning out far better than I had expected it to; it was good, very good. My confidence in my ability soared. I could paint, really paint. All I had to do was work at it, boldly but slowly.

Along with the ninth day, Helen, cramped by a long session got up and walked around the room shaking her arms and kicking her legs. I lit two cigarettes and handed her one. She put an arm around my waist and studied the painting for several minutes.

"This is me, Harry, only it looks like me when I was a little girl."

"I'm not finished yet. I've been working on the hands. I figure a good two days to finish your face. If possible I want to paint your lips the same shade as your lipstick, but if I do I'm afraid it'll look out of place. It's a tricky business."

"What about the background?"

"I'm letting that go. It isn't important."

"But the picture won't be complete without a background."

"I'm not going to fill the empty places with that gray wallpaper and its weird pattern of pink flowers!"

"You don't have to. Can't you paint in an open sky, or the ocean and clouds behind me?"

"No. That would look lousy. Wrong light, anyway."

"You can't leave it blank!"

"I can until I get an idea. If I have to fill it with something I can paint it orange with black spots."

"You can't do that! That would ruin it!"

"Then let's not discuss it any more."

It made me a little sore. A man who's painting a picture doesn't want a layman's advice. At least I didn't. This was the best thing of its kind I had ever done and I was going to do it my way.

That night when we went down to Mike's for dinner I started to drink again. Both of us were well-loaded when we got home and for the first time we went to sleep without making love.

I slept until noon. Helen didn't wake me when she went to the delicatessen for beer and whiskey. The coffee was perking in the pot and the wonderful odor woke me. I drank two cups of it black and had one shot of whiskey followed by a beer chaser. I felt fine.

"Today and tomorrow and I'll be finished," I told Helen confidently.

"I'm sure tired of that pose."

"You don't have to hold it any longer, baby. All I have to finish is your face."

I had overestimated the time it would take me. By three-thirty there was nothing more to do. Anything else I did to the painting would be plain fiddling. Maybe I hadn't put in a proper background, but I had captured Helen and that was what I had set out to do. Enough of the bed and the two pillows were showing to lend form and solidity to the composition. The girl in the portrait was Helen, a much younger Helen, and if possible, a much prettier and delicate Helen, but it was Helen as she appeared to me. Despite my attempts to create the faint, tiny lines around her eyes and the streak of silver hair, it was the portrait of a young girl.

"It's beautiful," Helen said sincerely and self-consciously.

"It's the best I can do."

"How much could you sell this for, Harry?"

"I wouldn't sell it. It belongs to you."

"But what would it be worth to an art gallery?"

"It's hard to tell. Whatever you could get, I suppose. Twenty dollars, maybe."

"Surely, more than that!"

"It all depends upon how much somebody wants it. That's the way art works. The artist has his asking price, of course, and if a buyer wants the painting he pays the price. If they don't want it he couldn't give the picture away. My price for this picture is one hundred thousand dollars."

"I'd pay that much for it, Harry."

"And so would I." There was a drink apiece left in the bottle of whiskey. We divided it equally and toasted the portrait.

"If I never paint another," I bragged, "I've painted one picture."

"It doesn't really need a background, Harry," Helen said loyally, "it looks better the way it is."

"You're wrong, but the hell with it. Get dressed and we'll go out and celebrate."

"Let's stay in instead," Helen said quietly.

"Why? If you're tired of drinking at Big Mike's we can go some place else. We don't have to go there."

"No, that isn't it," she said hesitantly. "We're all out of money, Harry." The corners of her mouth turned down wryly. "I spent the last cent I had for that bottle."

"Okay. So we're out of money. You didn't expect two hundred dollars to last forever did you? Our room rent's paid, anyway."

"Do you have any money, Harry?"

After searching through my wallet and my trousers I came up with two dollars and a half dollar in change. Not a large sum, but enough for a few drinks.

"This is enough for a couple at Mike's," I said, "or we can let the drinks go and I can look around for a job. It's up to you."

"I would like to have a drink . . . but while you're looking for work, and even after you find it, there'll still be several days before you get paid."

"We'll worry about that when we come to it. I've got fifteen dollars credit with Mike and it's all paid up. I paid him the other night when you cashed a traveler's check."

"We don't have a worry in the world then, do we?" Helen said brightly.

"Not one." I said it firmly, but with a confidence I didn't

feel inside. I had a lot of things to worry about. The smile was back on Helen's lips. She gave me a quick ardent kiss and dressed hurriedly, so fast I had to laugh.

When we got to Mike's we sat down in an empty booth and ordered hamburgers instead of our usual club steak. It was the only thing we had eaten all day, but it was still too much for me. After two bites I pushed my hamburger aside, left Helen in the booth, and signaled Mike to come down to the end of the bar.

"Mike," I said apprehensively, "I'm back on credit again."

"Okay." He nodded his massive head slowly. "I'm not surprised, though, the way you two been hitting it lately."

"I'm going to find a job tomorrow."

"You've always paid up, Harry. I'm not worried."

"Thanks, Mike." I turned to leave.

"Just a minute, Harry," he said seriously. "That guy you had a fight with the other night was in here earlier and I think he's looking for you. I ran him the hell out, but you'd better be on the lookout for him. His face looks pretty bad. There's about thirty stitches in his face and the way it's sewed up makes him look like he's smiling. Only he ain't smiling."

"I feel sorry for the guy, Mike. I don't know what got into me the other night."

"Well, I thought I'd better mention it."

"Thanks, Mike." I rejoined Helen in the booth. She had finished her sandwich and mine too.

"You didn't want it, did you?" she asked me.

I shook my head. We ordered whiskey with water chasers and stayed where we were, in the last booth against the wall, drinking until ten o'clock. I was in a mighty depressed mood and I unconsciously transmitted it to Helen. I should never have let her talk me into painting her portrait. I should never have tried any type of painting again. There was no use trying to kid myself that I could paint. Of course, the portrait was all right, but any artist with any academic background at all could have done as well. And my temerity in posing Helen as *Olympia* was the crowning height to my folly. Who in the hell did I think I was, anyway? What was I trying to prove? Liquor never helped me when I was in a depressed state of mind; it only made me feel worse. Helen broke the long, dead silence between us.

"This isn't much of a celebration, is it?"

"No. I guess not."

"Do you want to go home, Harry?"

"What do you want to do?"

"If I sit here much longer looking at you, I'll start crying."

"Let's go home, then."

I signed the tab that Tommy the waiter brought and we left. It was a dark, forbidding block to the roominghouse at night. Except for Big Mike's bar and grill on the corner, the light from Mr. Watson's delicatessen across the street was the only bright spot on the way home. We walked slowly, Helen holding onto my arm. Half-way up the street I stopped, fished two cigarettes out of my almost empty package and turned into the wind to light them. Helen accepted the lighted cigarette I handed her and inhaled deeply. We didn't know what to do with ourselves.

"What's ever to become of us, Harry?" Helen sighed.

"I don't know."

"Nothing seems to have much purpose, does it?"

"No, it doesn't."

A man I hadn't noticed in the darkness of the street, detached himself from the shadows of the Spotless Cleaner's storefront and walked toward us. His hat was pulled well down over his eyes and he was wearing a dark-brown topcoat. The faint light from the street lamp on the corner barely revealed a long red scar on his face and neat row of stitches. Like Mike had told me, the left corner of his mouth was pulled up unnaturally, and it made the man look like he was smiling.

With a quick movement he jerked a shiny, nickel-plated pistol out of his topcoat pocket and covered us with it. His hand was shaking violently and the muzzle of the pistol jerked up and down rapidly, as though it was keeping time to wild music.

"I've been waiting for you!" His voice was thick and muffled. His jaws were probably wired together and he was forced to talk through his teeth. I dropped my cigarette to the pavement and put my left arm protectingly around Helen's waist. She stared at the man with a dazed, fixed expression.

"I'm going to kill you," he said through his clenched teeth. "Both of you!"

"I don't blame you," I answered calmly. I felt no fear or anxiety at all, just a morbid feeling of detachment. Helen's body trembled beneath my arm, but it couldn't have been from fear, because the trembling stopped abruptly, and she took another deep drag on her cigarette.

"You may shoot me first, if you prefer," she said quietly.

"God damn the both of you!" the man said through his closed mouth. "Get down on your knees! Beg me! Beg for your lives!"

I shook my head. "No. We don't do that for anybody. Our lives aren't that important."

He stepped forward and jammed the muzzle into my stomach with a hard, vicious thrust.

"Pray, you son-of-a-bitch! Pray!"

I should have been frightened, but I wasn't. I knew that I should have been afraid and I even wondered why I wasn't.

"Go ahead," I told him. "Pull the trigger. I'm ready."

He hesitated and this hesitation, I believe, is what cost him his nerve. He backed slowly away from us, the pistol dancing in his hand, as though it had an independent movement of its own.

"You don't think I'll shoot you, do you?" It was the kind of a question for which there is no answer. We didn't reply.

"All right, bastard," he said softly, "start walking."

We started walking slowly up the sidewalk and he dodged to one side and fell in behind us. He jammed the pistol into the small of my back. I felt its pressure for ten or more steps and then it was withdrawn. Helen held my left arm with a tight grip, but neither one of us looked back as we marched up the hill. At any moment I expected a slug to tear through my body. We didn't look behind us until we reached the steps of the rooming house, and then I turned and looked over my shoulder while Helen kept her eyes straight to the front. There was no one in sight.

We entered the house, walked quietly down the dimly lighted hallway, and went into our room. I closed the door, turned on the light, and Helen sat down on the edge of the bed. Conscious of Helen's eyes on me, I walked across to the painting and examined it for a long time.

"Did you feel sorry for him, Harry? I did."

"Yes, I did," I replied sincerely. "The poor bastard."

"I don't believe I'd have really cared if he'd killed us both . . ." Helen's voice was reflective, somber.

"Cared?" I forced a tight smile. "It would have been a favor."

suicide pact 6

There was something bothering me when I got out of bed the next morning. I had a queasy, uneasy feeling in the pit of my stomach and it took me a few minutes to figure out what caused it. It was early in the morning, much too early to be getting out of bed. The sun was just coming up and the light filtering through the window was gray and cold. The sky was matted with low clouds, but an occasional bright spear broke through to stab at the messy backyards and the littered alley extending up the hill. I turned away from the window and the dismal view that looked worse by sunlight than it did by night.

I filled the coffee pot with water and put it on the burner. I took the coffee can down from the shelf above the sink and opened it. The coffee can was empty. I turned the fire out under the pot. No coffee this morning. I searched through my pockets before I put my trousers on and didn't find a dime. I didn't expect to, but I looked anyway. Not only had I spent the two and a half dollars in change, I had signed a chit besides for the drinks we had at Mike's. I opened Helen's purse and searched it thoroughly. There wasn't any money, but the purse contained a fresh, unopened package of cigarettes. After I finished dressing I sat in the straight chair by the window, smoking until Helen awoke.

Helen awoke after three cigarettes, sat up in bed and stretched her arms widely. She never yawned or appeared drowsy when she awoke in the mornings, but always appeared to be alert and fresh, as though she didn't need the sleep at all.

"Good morning, darling," she said. "How about lighting me one of those?"

I lit a fresh cigarette from the end of mine, put it between her lips, and sat down on the edge of the bed.

"No kiss?" she said petulantly, taking the cigarette out of her mouth. I kissed her and then returned to my chair by the window.

"We're out of coffee," I said glumly.

"That isn't such a great calamity, is it?"

"We're out of money too. Remember?"

"We've got credit, haven't we? Let's go down to Big Mike's for coffee. He might put a shot of bourbon in it if we ask him real nice."

"You really feel good, don't you?" I said bitterly.

Helen got out of bed and padded barefoot over to my chair. She put her arms around my neck, sat in my lap and kissed me on the neck.

"Look out," I said. "You'll burn me with your cigarette."

"No, I won't. And I don't feel a bit good. I feel rotten."

She bit me sharply on the ear, dropped her slip over her head and departed for the bathroom next door. I left my chair to examine my painting in the cold light of early morning. I twisted the easel around so the picture would face the window. A good amateur or Sunday painter would be proud of that portrait, I decided. Why wasn't I the one artist in a thousand who could earn his living by painting? Of course, I could always go back to teaching. Few men in the painting world knew as much as I did about color. The coarse thought of teaching made me shudder with revulsion. If you can't do it yourself you tell someone else how to do it. You stand behind them in the role of peer and mentor and watch them get better and better. You watch them overshadow you until you are nothing except a shadow within a shadow and then lost altogether in the unequal merger. Perhaps that was my main trouble? I could bring out talent where there wasn't any talent. Where there wasn't any ability I could bring out the semblance of ability. A fine quality for a man born to teach, but a heartbreaking quality for a man born to be an artist. No, I would never teach again. There were too many art students who thought they were artists who should have been mechanics. But a teacher was never allowed to be honest and tell them to quit. The art schools would have very few students if the teachers were allowed to be honest. But then, didn't the same thing hold true for all schools?

I threw myself across the bed and covered my ears with my hands. I didn't want to think about it any more. I didn't want to think about anything. Helen returned from the bathroom and curled up beside me on the bed.

"What's the matter, darling?" she asked solicitously. "Have you got a headache?"

"No. I was just thinking what a rotten, stinking world this is we live in. This isn't our kind of world, Helen. And we don't have the answer to it either. We aren't going to beat it by drinking and yet, the only way we can possibly face it is by drinking!"

"You're worried because we don't have any money, aren't you?"

"Not particularly."

"I could wire my mother for money if you want me to."

"Do you think she'd send it?"

"She'd probably bring it! She doesn't know where I am and I don't want her to know. But we're going to have to get money someplace."

"Why?"

"You need a cup of coffee and I need a drink. That's why."

"I don't give a damn about the coffee. Why do you have to have a drink? You don't really need it."

"Sure I do. I'm an alcoholic. Alcoholics drink."

"Suppose you were dead? You'd never need another drink. You wouldn't need anything. Everything would be blah. It doesn't make you happy to drink, and when I drink it only makes me unhappier than I am already. All it does in the long run is bring us oblivion."

"I need you when I come out of that oblivion, Harry." Her voice was solemn and barely under control.

"I need you too, Helen." This was as true a statement as I had ever made. Without Helen I was worse than nothing, a dark, faceless shadow, alone in the darkness. I had to take her with me.

"I haven't thought about suicide in a long time, Helen," I said. "Not once since we've been together. I used to think about it all of the time, but I never had the nerve. Together, maybe we could do it. I know I couldn't do it alone."

"I used to think about suicide too." Helen accepted my mood and took it for her own. "Down in San Sienna. It was such a tight, hateful little town. My bedroom overlooked the ocean, and I'd sit there all day, with the door locked, curled up on the window-seat, hiding my empty bottles in my dirty clothes hamper. Sitting there like that, looking at the golden sunshine glistening on the water, watching the breakers as they crashed on the beach . . . It made me depressed as hell. It was all so purposeless!"

"Did you ever attempt it?"

"Suicide?"

"That's what we're considering. Suicide."

"Yes, I tried it once." She smiled wryly. "On my wedding night, Harry. I was still a virgin, believe it or not. Oh, I wasn't ignorant; I knew what was expected of me and I thought I was ready for it. But I wasn't. Not for what happened, anyway. It was a virtual onslaught! My husband was a real estate man, and I'd never seen him in anything except a suit—all dressed up you know, with a clean, respectable look.

"But all of a sudden—I was in bed first, wearing my new nightgown, and shivering with apprehension—he flew out of the bathroom without a stitch on and rushed across the room. He was actually gibbering and drooling at the mouth. He tore the covers off me. He ripped my new, nice nightgown to shreds . . ." Helen's voice broke as she relived this experience and she talked with difficulty. "I fought him. I tore at his face with my nails; I bit him, hit at him, but it didn't make any difference. I'm positive now, that that's what he wanted me to do, you see. He overpowered me easily and completely. Then, in a second, it was all over. I was raped. He walked casually into the bathroom, doctored his scratches with iodine, put his pajamas on and climbed into bed as though nothing had happened."

Helen smiled grimly, crushed her cigarette in the ashtray.

"It was his first and last chance at me," she continued. "I never gave him another. Lying there beside him in the darkness I vowed that he'd never touch me again. After he was asleep I got out of bed and took the bottle of aspirins out of my overnight bag and went into the bathroom. There were twenty-six tablets. I counted them, because I didn't know for sure whether that was enough or not. But I decided it was and I took them three at a time until they were gone, washing each bunch down with a glass of water. Then I climbed back into bed—"

"That wasn't nearly enough," I said, interested in her story.

"No, it wasn't. But I fell asleep though, and I probably wouldn't have otherwise. They must have had some kind of psychological effect. But I awoke the next morning the same as ever, except for a loud ringing in my ears. The ringing lasted all day."

"What about your husband? Did he know you attempted suicide?"

"I didn't give him that satisfaction. We were staying at a beach motel in Santa Barbara, and after breakfast he went out to the country club to play golf. I begged off—told him I wanted to do some shopping—and as soon as he drove away I packed my bag and caught a bus for San Sienna and Mother. Mother was glad to have me back."

"And you never went back to him?"

"Never. I told Mother what happened. It was foolish of me, maybe, but she was determined to find out so I told her about it. Later on, when he begged me to come back to him, I was going to, but she wouldn't let me. He didn't know any better, the poor guy, and he told me so, after he found out the reason I left him. But it was too late then. I was safe in Mother's arms."

She finished her story bitterly, and her features assumed the tragic look I knew so well, the look that entered her face whenever she mentioned her mother. I kissed her tenderly on the mouth, got out of bed, and paced the floor restlessly.

"I'm glad you told me about this, Helen. That's when you started to drink, isn't it?"

"Yes, that's when I started to drink. It was as good an excuse as any other."

We were silent then, deep in our own thoughts. Helen lay on her back with her eyes closed while I paced the floor. I understood Helen a little better now. Thanks to me, and I don't know how many others, she didn't feel the same way about sex now, but she was so fixed in her drinking habits she could never change them. Not without some fierce drive from within, and she wasn't made that way. Before she could ever stop drinking she would have to have some purpose to her life, and I couldn't furnish it. Not when I didn't even have a purpose for my own life. If we continued on, in the direction we were traveling, the only thing that could possibly happen would be a gradual lowering of standards and they were low enough already. If something happened to me she would end up on the streets of San Francisco. The very thought of this sent a cold chill down my back. And I couldn't take care of her properly. It was too much of an effort to take care of myself . . .

"It takes a lot of nerve to commit suicide, Harry," Helen said suddenly, sitting up in bed, and swinging her feet to the floor.

"If we did it together I think we could do it," I said confidently. "Right now, we're on the bottom rung of the ladder. We're dead broke. I haven't got a job, and there's no one we can turn to for help. No whiskey, no religion, nothing."

"Do you think we'd be together afterwards?"

"Are you talking about the hereafter?"

"That's what I mean. I wouldn't care whether I went to Heaven or Hell as long as I was with you."

"I don't know anything about those things, Helen. But here's the way I look at it. If we went together, we'd be together. I'm positive of that."

The thought of death was very attractive to me. I could tell by the fixed expression in Helen's eyes that she was in the same mood I was in. She got the cigarettes from the table and sat down again on the edge of the bed. After she lit the cigarettes, I took mine and sat down beside her.

"How would we go about it, Harry?" Helen was in earnest, but her voice quavered at her voiced thought.

"There are lots of ways."

"But how, though? I can't stand being hurt. If it was all over with like that—" she snapped her fingers— "and I didn't feel anything, I think I could do it."

"We could cut our wrists with a razor blade."

"Oh, no!" She shuddered. "That would hurt terribly!"

"No it wouldn't," I assured her. "Just for one second, maybe, and then it would all be over."

"I couldn't do it, Harry!" She shook her head emphatically. "If you did it for me I could shut my eyes and—"

"No!" I said sharply. "You'll have to do it yourself. If I cut your wrists, well, then it would be murder. That's what it would be."

"Not if I asked you to."

"No. We'll have to do it together."

When we finished our cigarettes I put the ashtray back on the table. I was serious about committing suicide and determined to go through with it. There wasn't any fight left in me. As far as I was concerned the world we existed on was an overly-large, stinking cinder, a spinning, useless clinker. I didn't want any part of it. My life meant nothing to me and I wanted to go to sleep forever and forget about it. I got my shaving kit down from the shelf above the sink and took the package of razor blades out of it. I unwrapped the waxed paper from two shiny single-edged blades and laid them on the table. Helen joined me at the table and held out her left arm dramatically.

"Go ahead," she said tearfully. "Cut it!"

Her eyes were tightly squeezed shut and she was breathing rapidly. I took her hand in mine and looked at her thin little wrist. I almost broke down and it was an effort to fight back the tears.

"No, sweetheart," I said to her gently, "you'll have to do it yourself. I can't do it for you."

"Which one is mine?" she asked nervously.

"Either one. It doesn't make any difference."

"Are you going to give a signal?" She picked up a blade awkwardly.

"I'll count to three." I picked up the remaining blade.

"I'm ready!" she said bravely, raising her chin.

"One. Two. Three!"

We didn't do anything. We just stood there, looking at each other.

"It's no use, Harry. I can't do it to myself." She threw the blade down angrily on the table and turned away. She covered her face with her hands and sobbed. Her back shook convulsively.

"Do you want me to do it?" I asked her.

She nodded her head almost imperceptibly, but she didn't say anything. I jerked her left hand away from her face and with one quick decisive motion I cut blindly into her wrist. She screamed sharply, then compressed her lips, and held out her other arm. I cut it quickly, close to the heel of her hand, picked her up and carried her to the bed. I arranged a pillow under her head.

"Do they hurt much?"

She shook her head. "They burn a little bit. That's all."

Her eyes were closed, but she was still crying noiselessly. The bright blood gushed from her wrists, making crimson pools on the white sheets. I retrieved the bloody blade from the table where I'd dropped it, returned to the bed and sat down. It was much more difficult to cut my own wrists. The skin was tougher, somehow, and I had to saw with the blade to cut through. My heart was beating so loud I could feel it throb through my body. I was afraid to go through with it and afraid not to go through with it. The blood frothed finally, out of my left wrist and I transferred the blade to my other hand. It was easier to cut my right wrist, even though I was right-handed. It didn't hurt nearly as much as I had expected it to, but there was a searing, burning sensation, as though I had inadvertently touched my wrists to a hot poker. I threw the blade to the floor and got into bed beside Helen. She kissed me passionately. I could feel the life running out of my wrists and it made me happy and excited.

"Harry?"

"Yes?"

"As a woman I'd like to have the last word. Is it all right?"

"Sure it's all right."

"I. Love. You."

It was the first time she had said the word since we had been living together. I kissed each of her closed eyes tenderly, then buried my face in her neck. I was overwhelmed with emotion and exhaustion.

return to life 7

My head was like a huge bubble perched on top of my shoulders, and ready for instant flight. I was afraid to move my head or open my eyes for fear it would float away into nothingness. Gradually, as I lay there fearfully, a feeling of solidity returned to my head and I opened my eyes. My arms were entwined around Helen, and she was lying on her side, facing me, her breathing soft and regular, in deep, restful sleep—but she was breathing! We were still alive, very much so! I disentangled my arms and raised my wrists so that I could see them. The blood was coagulated into little black ridges along the lengths of the shallow cuts. The bleeding had completely stopped. Oddly enough, I felt highly exhilarated and happy to be alive. It was as though I was experiencing a "cheap" drink; I felt the way I had when I had taken a lower lip full of snuff many years before. My head was light and I was a trifle dizzy even though I was still in bed. I awakened Helen by kissing her partly open mouth. For a moment her eyes were startled and then they brightened into alertness the way they always did when she first awakened. She smiled shyly.

"I guess I didn't cut deep enough," I said ruefully. "I must have missed the arteries altogether."

"How do you feel, Harry?" Helen asked me. "I feel kind of wonderful, sort of giddy."

"I feel a little foolish. And at the same time I feel better than I have in months. I'm light-headed as hell and I feel drunk. Not gin-drunk, but drunk with life."

"I feel the same way. I've never been as drunk as I am now and I haven't had a drink. I never expected to wake up at all—not here, anyway."

"Neither did I," I said quietly.

"Are you sorry, Harry?"

"No. I'm not exactly sorry. It's too easy to quit and yet it took me a long time to reach the point when I was ready. But now that I've tried it once I guess I can face things again. It's still a lousy world, but maybe we owe it something."

"Light us a cigarette, Harry."

I got out of bed carefully and staggered dizzily to the table. I picked up the package of cigarettes and a folder of book matches and then noticed the bloody razor blade on the floor. It was unreal and cruel-looking and somehow offended me. I scooped it off the floor with the edge of the cardboard match folder and dropped it into the paper sack where we kept our trash and garbage. I couldn't bear to touch it with my hands. I was so giddy by this time it was difficult to keep my feet. Tumbling back onto the bed I lit Helen's cigarette, then mine.

"You've got a surprise coming when you try to walk," I said.

"You were actually staggering," Helen said, dragging the smoke deeply into her lungs.

"This bed is certainly a mess. Take a look at it."

"We'd better burn these sheets. I don't think the laundry would take them like this." Helen giggled.

"That is, if we could afford to take them to the laundry."

Both of us were in a strange mood, caused mostly by the blood we had lost. It wasn't a gay mood, not exactly, but it wasn't depressed either. All of our problems were still with us, but for a brief moment, out of mind. There was still no money, no job, no liquor and no prospects. I was still a bit light-headed and it was hard for me to think about our many problems. I wished, vaguely, that I had a religion or a God of some sort. It would have been so wonderful and easy to have gone to a priest or a minister and let him solve our problems for us. We could have gone anyway, religious or not, but without faith, any advice we listened to would have been worthless. The pat, standard homilies dished out by the boys in black were easy to predict.

Accept Jesus Christ as your personal Lord and Saviour and you are saved!

Any premise which bases its salvation on blind belief alone is bound to be wrong, I felt. It isn't fair to those who find it impossible to believe, those who have to be convinced, shown, who believe in nothing but the truth. But, all the same, suppose we did go to a church somewhere? What could we lose?

I rejected that false line of reasoning in a hurry.

"Let's bandage each other's wrists," I said quickly to Helen. It would at least be something to do. I left the bed and sat down for a moment in the straight chair by the easel.

"I suppose we'd better," Helen agreed, "before they get infected. If we're going to burn these sheets anyway, why don't you tear a few strips from the edge? They'll make fine bandages." Helen got out of bed wearily and walked in tight circles, trying her legs. "Boy, am I dizzy!" she exclaimed, and sat down on the foot of the bed.

I tore several strips of sheeting from the top sheet. Helen did some more circles and then sat down in a chair and fanned herself with her hands. I patted her bare shoulder reassuringly on my way to the dresser. My giddiness had all but disappeared, but my feeling of exhilaration remained. I had to dig through every drawer in the dresser before I could find the package of band-aids.

"Hold out your arms," I told Helen. The gashes in her wrists hurt me to look at them. They were much deeper than my own and the tiny blue veins in her thin wrists were closer to the surface than they had been before. I was deeply ashamed, and bound her wrists rapidly with the sheeting. I used the band-aids to hold the improvised bandages in place and then we changed places. She bandaged my wrists while I sat in the chair, but did a much neater job of it.

Without warning Helen rushed into my arms and began to sob uncontrollably. Her slender back was racked with violent, shuddering sobs and her hot flush of tears burned on my bare chest. I tried my best to comfort her.

"There, there, old girl," I said crooningly, "this won't do at all. Don't cry, baby, everything's going to be all right. There, there . . ."

She continued to sob piteously for a long time and all I could do was hold her. I was helpless, confused. It wasn't like Helen to cry about anything. At last she calmed down, smiled weakly, and wiped her streaming eyes with her fingers, like a little girl.

"I know it's childish of me, Harry, to cry like that, but I couldn't help it. The thought exploded inside my head and caught me when I wasn't expecting it."

"What did, honey?"

"Well, suppose you had died and I hadn't? And I woke up, and there you were—dead, and there I'd be, alone, still alive, without you, without anything . . ." Her tears started to flow again, but with better restraint. I held her on my lap like a frightened child; her face against my shoulder. I made no attempts to prevent her silent crying. I just patted her gently on her bare back, letting her cry it out. I knew precisely how she felt, because my feelings were exactly the same. Within a few minutes she was calm again and smiling her secret, tragic smile.

"If you'd kept up much longer I'd have joined you," I said, attempting a smile.

"Do you know what's the matter with us, Harry?"

"Everything. Just name it."

"No." She shook her head. "We've lost our perspective. What we need is help, psychiatric help."

"At fifty bucks an hour, we can't afford one second of help."

"We can go to a hospital."

"That costs even more."

"Not a public hospital."

"Well, there's Saint Paul's, but I'm leery of it."

"Why? Is it free?" she asked eagerly.

"Sure, it's free all right, but what if they decide we're nuts and lock us up in a state institution for a few years? You in a woman's ward, me in a men's ward?"

"Oh, they wouldn't do that, Harry. We aren't crazy. This wholesale depression we're experiencing is caused strictly by alcohol. If we can get a few drugs and a little conversation from a psychiatrist, we'll be just fine again. I'll bet they wouldn't keep us more than a week at the longest."

"That isn't the way it works, baby," I told her. "A psychiatrist isn't a witch doctor with a speedy cure for driving out the devils. It's a long process, as I understand it, and the patient really cures himself. All the psychiatrist can do is help him along by guiding the thinking a little bit. He listens and says nothing. He doesn't even give the patient any sympathy. All he does is listen."

"That doesn't make any sense to me."

"But that's the way it works."

"Well . . ." She thought for a few moments. "They could get us off the liquor couldn't they?"

"If we didn't have any, and couldn't get any, yes. But even there, you have to have a genuine desire to quit drinking."

"I don't want to drink anymore, Harry. Let's take a chance on it, to see what happens. We can't lose anything, and I know they aren't going to lock us up anywhere, because it costs the state too much money for that. Both of us need some kind of help right now, and you know it!"

I caught some of Helen's enthusiasm, but for a different reason. The prospect of a good rest, a chance to sleep at night, some proper food in my stomach appealed to me. It was a place to start from . . .

"A week wouldn't be so bad at that," I said. "I could get straightened around some, maybe do a little thinking. I might come up with an idea."

"I could too, Harry. There are lots of things we could do together! You know all about art. Why, I'll bet we could start an art gallery and make a fortune right here in San Francisco! Did you ever get your G.I. loan?"

"No."

"A veteran can borrow all kinds of money! I think they loan as high as four thousand dollars."

"Maybe so, but an art gallery isn't any good. The dealers are all starving to death, even the well-established ones. People don't buy decent pictures for their homes any more. They buy pictures in the same place they get their new furniture. If the frame matches the davenport, they buy the picture, no matter what it is. No art gallery for me."

"They give business loans too."

"They may not take us in at the hospital." I brought the subject back to the business at hand.

"If we show them our wrists, I'll bet they'll take us in!"

I knew that Helen was right and yet I was afraid to turn in to Saint Paul's Hospital. But I could think of nothing better to do. Maybe a few days of peace and quiet were all we needed. I could use a new outlook on life. It was the smart thing to do, and for once in my life, why couldn't I do the smart thing?

"All right, Helen. Get dressed. We'll try it. If they take us in, fine! If they don't, they can go to hell."

After we were dressed, Helen began to roll up the bloody sheets to take them out to the incinerator. "Just a second," I said, and I tossed my box of oil paints and the rest of my painting equipment into the middle of the pile of sheets. "Burn that junk, too," I told her.

"You don't want to burn your paints!"

"Just do what I tell you. I know what I'm doing."

While Helen took the bundle out to the backyard to burn it in the incinerator, I walked down the hall to Mrs. McQuade's room and knocked on her door.

"Mrs. McQuade," I said, when she answered my insistent rapping. "My wife and I are going out of town for a few days. We're going to visit her mother down in San Sienna."

"How many days will you be gone, Mr. Jordan?" she asked suspiciously.

"I'm not sure yet. About a week, maybe not that long."

"I can't give you any refund, Mr. Jordan. You didn't give me any advance notice."

"I didn't ask for a refund, Mrs. McQuade."

"I know you didn't, but I thought it best to mention it." She fluttered her apron and smiled pleasantly. "Now you go ahead and have a nice time. Your room'll still be here when you get back."

"We will," I said grimly. "We expect to have a grand old time."

I returned to the room. Helen was packing her suitcase with her night things, cold cream, and toothbrush. All I took was my shaving kit. As we left the room she handed me the suitcase and locked the door with her key. At the bottom of the steps, outside in the street, I gave her my leather shaving kit to carry so I could have one hand free.

"How do you feel, baby?" I asked Helen as we paused in front of the house.

"A wee bit dizzy still, but otherwise I'm all right. Why?"

"We've got a long way ahead of us, that's why." I grinned. "We don't have enough change for carfare."

"Oh!" She lifted her chin bravely. "Then let's get started," she said resolutely, looking into my eyes.

I shrugged my shoulders, Helen took my arm, and we started walking up the hill.

hospital case 8

San Francisco is an old city with old buildings, and it is built on seven ancient hills. And long before Helen and I reached the grounds of Saint Paul's Hospital it seemed as though we had climbed every one of them. The narrow, twisted streets, the weathered, brown and crumbling façades of the rotted, huddled buildings frowning upon us as we labored up and down the hills, gave me poignant, bitter memories of my neighborhood in early childhood days: Chicago's sprawling South Side. There was no particular resemblance between the two cities I could put my finger on, but the feeling of similarity persisted. Pausing at the crest of a long, steep hill for rest and breath, I saw the magnificent panorama of the great harbor spreading below us. Angel Island, Alcatraz, several rusty, vagrant ships, a portion of the Golden Gate, and the land mass of Marin County, San Francisco's bedroom, were all within my vision at one time. The water of the bay, a dark and Prussian blue, was the only link with Chicago and my past.

The long walk was good for me. I saw a great many things I had been merely looking at for a long time. It was as though I was seeing the city through new eyes, for the first time.

The late, slanting, afternoon sun made long, fuzzy shadows; dark, colored shadows that dragged from the tops of the buildings like old-fashioned cloaks.

Noisy children were playing in the streets, shouting, screaming, laughing; all of them unaware of money and security and death.

Bright, shiny, new automobiles, chromium-trimmed, two-toned and silent, crept bug-like up and down the steep street. How long had it been since I had owned an automobile? I couldn't remember.

House-wives in house-dresses, their arms loaded with groceries in brown-paper sacks, on their way home to prepare dinner for their working husbands. How long had it been since I had had a home? I had never had a home.

I saw non-objective designs created with charm and simplicity on every wall, every fence, every puddle of water we passed; the designs of unconscious forms and colors, patterns waiting to be untrapped by an artist's hand. The many-hued spot of oil and water surrounded by blue-black macadam. The tattered, blistered, peeling ochre paint, stripping limply from a redwood wall of an untenanted house. The clean, black spikes of ornamental iron-work fronting a narrow stucco beauty-shop. Arranged for composition and drawn in soft pastels, what delicate pictures these would be for a young girl's bedroom. For Helen's bedroom. For our bedroom. If we had a house and a bedroom and a kitchen and a living-room and a dining-room and maybe another bedroom and I had a job and I was among the living once again and I was painting again and neither one of us was drinking . . .

> In a dim corner of my room for longer than my
> fancy thinks
> A beautiful and silent Sphinx has watched me
> through the shifting gloom.

"Let's sit down for a while, Harry," Helen said wearily. There was a bus passenger's waiting bench nearby, and we both sat down. I took the shaving kit out of Helen's lap and put it inside the suitcase. No reason for her to carry it when there was room inside the suitcase. She was more tired than I was. She smiled wanly and patted my hand.

"Do you know what I've been thinking about, Harry?"

"No, but I've been thinking all kinds of things."

"It may be too early to make plans, Harry, but after we get out of the hospital and get some money again I'm going to get a divorce. It didn't make any difference before and it still doesn't—not the way I feel about you, I mean, but I'd like to be married to you. Legally, I mean."

"Why legally?"

"There isn't any real reason. I feel that I'd like it better and so would you."

"I like things better the way they are," I said, trying to discourage her. "Marriage wouldn't make me feel any different. But if it would make you any happier, that's what we'll do. But now is no time to talk about it."

"I know. First off, I'll have to get a divorce."

"That isn't hard. Where's your husband now?"

"Somewhere in San Diego, I think. I could find him. His parents are still living in San Sienna."

"Well, let's not talk about it now, baby. We've got plenty of time. Right now I'm concerned with getting hospital treatment for whatever's the matter with me, if there is such a thing, and there's anything the matter with me. What do you say?"

"I'm rested." Helen got to her feet. "Want me to carry the suitcase a while?"

"Of course not."

Saint Paul's hospital is a six-story building set well back from the street and surrounded by an eight-foot cyclone wire fence. In front of the hospital a small park of unkempt grass, several rows of geraniums, and a few antlered, unpruned elms are the only greenery to be seen for several blocks. The hospital stands like a red, sore finger in the center of a residential district; a section devoted to four-unit duplexes and a fringe of new ranch-style apartment hotels. Across the street from the entrance-way a new shopping-center and parking lot stretches half-way down the block. As we entered the unraked gravel path leading across the park to the receiving entrance, Helen's tired feet lagged. When we reached the thick, glass double-doors leading into the lobby, she stopped and squeezed my hand.

"Are you sure you want to go through with this, Harry?" she asked me anxiously. "We didn't really have a chance to talk it over much. It was a kind of a spur-of-the-moment decision and we don't have to go through with it. Not if you don't want to," she finished lamely.

"I'm not going to walk the three miles back to the roominghouse," I said. I could see the tiny cylinders clicking inside her head. "You're scared aren't you?"

"A little bit," she admitted. Her voice was husky. "Sure I am."

"They won't hurt us. It'll be a nice week's vacation," I assured her.

"Well . . . we've come this far . . ."

I pushed open the door and we timidly entered. The lobby was large and deep and the air was filled with a sharp, antiseptic odor that made my nose burn. There were many well-worn leather chairs scattered over the brown linoleum floor, most of them occupied with incoming and out-going patients, with their poverty showing in their faces and eyes. In the left corner of the room there was a waist-high circular counter encircling two green, steel desks. Standing behind the desk, instead of the usual bald hotel clerk, was a gray-faced nurse in a white uniform so stiff with starch she couldn't have bent down to tie her shoe-laces. The austere expression on her face was so stern, a man with a broken leg would have denied having it; he would have been afraid she might want to minister to it. We crossed the room to the counter.

"Hello," I said tentatively to her unsmiling face, as I set the suitcase on the floor. "We'd like to see a doctor about admittance to the hospital . . . a psychiatrist, if possible."

"Been here before?"

"No, ma'am."

"Which one of you is entering the hospital?"

"Both of us." I took another look at her gray face. "Maybe we are, I mean. We don't have a dime."

"The money isn't the important thing. If you can pay, we charge, naturally, but if you can't, that's something else again. What seems to be the trouble?"

I looked at Helen, but she looked away, examined the yellowing leaves of a sickly potted plant with great interest. I was embarrassed. It was such a silly thing we had done I hated to blurt it out to the nurse, especially such a practical-minded nurse. I was afraid to tell her for fear she would deliver a lecture of some sort. I forced myself to say it.

"We attempted suicide. We cut our wrists." I stretched my arms over the counter so she could see my bandaged wrists.

"And now you want to see a psychiatrist? Is that right?"

"Yes, ma'am. We thought we would. We need help."

"Come here, dear," the nurse said to Helen, with a sudden change in manner. "Let me see your wrists."

Helen, blushing furiously, pulled the sleeves off her jacket back and held out her wrists to the nurse. At that moment I didn't like myself very well. It was my fault Helen was going through this degrading experience. I had practically forced her into the stupid suicide pact. The nurse deftly unwrapped the clumsy bandages I had affixed to Helen's wrists. She gave me an amused, professional smile.

"Did you fix these?"

"Yes, ma'am. You see, we were in a hurry to get here and I wrapped them rather hastily," I explained.

The nurse puckered her lips and examined the raw wounds on Helen's slender wrists. She clucked sympathetically and handed each of us a three-by-five card and pencils. "Suppose you two sit over there and fill in these cards," she waved us to a decrepit lounge, "and we'll see what we shall see."

We sat down with the cards and Helen asked me in a whisper whether we should use our right names or not. I nodded and we filled in the cards with our names, addresses, etc. The nurse talked on her telephone, so quietly we couldn't hear the conversation from where we were sitting. In a few minutes a young, earnest-faced man, wearing white trousers and a short-sleeved white jacket got out of the elevator and walked directly to the desk. His feet, much too large for his short, squat body, looked larger than they were in heavy white shoes. He held a whispered conversation with the nurse, nodding his head gravely up and down in agreement. He crossed to our lounge and pulled a straight chair around so it faced us. He sat down on the edge of the chair.

"I am Doctor Davidson," he said briskly, unsmilingly. "We're going to admit you both to the hospital. But first of all you will have to sign some papers. The nurse tells me you have no money. Is that correct?"

"Yes, that is correct," I said. Helen said nothing. She kept her eyes averted from the doctor's face.

"The papers will be a mere formality, then." His face was

quite expressionless. I had a hunch that he practiced his blank expression in the mirror whenever he had the chance. He held out his hand for our filled-in cards. "Come with me, please," he ordered. He arose from his chair, dropped the cards on the counter, and marched quickly to the elevator without looking back. We trailed in his wake. At the sixth floor we got out of the elevator, walked to the end of the corridor, and he told us to sit down in two metal folding chairs against the wall. We sat for a solid hour, not talking, and afraid to smoke because there weren't any ashtrays. A young, dark-haired nurse came to Helen, crooked her finger.

"I want you to come with me, dear," she said to Helen.

"Where am I going?" Helen asked nervously.

"To the women's ward." The nurse smiled pleasantly.

"I thought we were going to be together—" Helen tried to protest.

"I'm sorry, dear, but that's impossible."

"What'll I do, Harry?" Helen turned to me helplessly.

"You'd better go with her, I guess. Let me get my shaving kit out of the bag." I opened the suitcase, retrieved my shaving kit, snapped the bag shut. "Go on with her, sweetheart, we've come this far, we might as well go through with it."

The nurse picked up the light over-nighter and Helen followed reluctantly, looking back at me all the way down the corridor. They turned a corner, disappeared from view, and I was alone on my metal folding chair.

In a few minutes Dr. Davidson returned for me and we went down the hall in the opposite direction. We entered his office and he handed me a printed form and told me to sign it. I glanced through the fine print perfunctorily, without reading it in detail. It was a form declaring that I was a pauper. There was no denying that. I signed the paper and shoved it across the desk.

"You're entering the hospital voluntarily, aren't you?" he asked.

"That's about it."

"Fill out these forms then." He handed me three different forms in three different colors. "You can use my office to fill them out." He left the office and I looked at the printed forms. There were questions about everything; my life's history, my health, my relative's health, my schooling, and anything else the hospital would never need to know. For a moment I considered filling them in, but not seriously. I took the desk pen and made a check mark beside each of the numbered questions on all of the forms. That would show that I had read the questions, and if they didn't like it the hell with them. I didn't want to enter the hospital anyway. The doctor returned in about a half an hour and I signed the forms in his presence. Without looking at them he shoved them into a brown manila folder.

"I'm going to be your doctor while you're here," he told me in his well-rehearsed impersonal manner, "but it'll be a couple of days before I can get to you. Let me see your wrists."

I extended my arms and he snipped the bandages loose with a pair of scissors, dropped the soiled sheeting into the waste-basket by his desk.

"What exactly brought this on, Jordan, or do you know?"

"We've been drinking for quite a while and we ran out of money. I suppose that's the main reason. Not that I'm an alcoholic or anything like that, but I'm out of work at present and I got depressed. Helen, more or less—"

"You mean, Mrs. Jordan?"

"No. Mrs. Meredith. Helen Meredith. We don't happen to be married, we're just living together, but we're going to be married later on. As I was saying, Helen takes my moods as hard as I do. If it hadn't been for me—well, this is all strictly my fault."

"We aren't concerned with whose fault it is, Jordan. Our job is to make you well. Do you want a drink now?"

"I could stand one all right."

"Do you feel like you need one?"

"No. I guess not."

"We'll let the drink go then. Hungry?"

"No. Not a bit."

He stood up, patted me on the shoulder, trying to be friendly. "After we take care of those cuts we'll give you some soup, and I'll have the nurse give you a little something that'll make you sleep."

We left his office and I followed him down the corridor to

Ward 3-C. There was a heavy, mesh-wire entrance door and
a buzzer set into the wall at the right. Dr. Davidson pressed
the buzzer and turned me over to an orderly he addressed
as Conrad. Conrad dressed my wrists and assigned me to a
bed. He issued me a pair of gray flannel pajamas, a blue
corduroy robe, and a pair of skivvy slippers. The skivvy
slippers were too large for me and the only way I could
keep them on was to shuffle my feet without lifting them
from the floor. He kept my shaving kit, locked it in a metal
cupboard by his desk, which was at the end of the ward.

I sat down on the edge of my bed and looked around the
ward. There were twenty-six beds and eleven men including myself. They all looked normal enough to me; none of
them looked or acted crazy. The windows were all barred,
however, with one-inch bars. I knew I was locked in, but I
didn't feel like a prisoner. It was more frightening than jail.
A man in jail knows what to expect. Here, I didn't.

Conrad brought me a bowl of weak vegetable soup, a
piece of bread and an apple on a tray. He set the tray on my
bedside stand.

"See what you can do to this," he said.

I spooned the soup down, not wanting it, but because I
thought the doctor wanted me to have it. I ignored the
apple and the piece of bread. When he came for the tray, he
brought me some foul-tasting lavender medicine in a shot
glass and I drank it. He took the tray, and said over his
shoulder as he left, "You d better hop into bed, boy. That
stuff'll hit you fast. It's a legitimate Mickey."

I removed my skivvy slippers and robe and climbed into
bed. It was soft and high and the sheets were like warm
snow. The sun was going down and its softly fading glow
came through the windows like a warm good-night kiss.
The light bulbs in the ceiling, covered with heavy wire
shields, glowed dully, without brightness. I fell asleep
almost at once, my head falling down and down into the
depths of my pillow.

It was three days before I talked to Dr. Davidson again.

shock treatment

After getting used to it, and it is easy, a neuro-psychiatric ward can be in its own fashion a rather satisfying world within a world. It is the security. Not the security of being locked in, but the security of having everything locked out. The security that comes from the sense of no responsibility for anything. In a way, it is kind of wonderful.

And there is the silence, the peace and the quiet of the ward. The other patients kept to themselves and so did I. One of the orderlies, Conrad or Jones, brought our razors in the morning and watched us while we shaved. I would take a long, hot shower and then make my bed. That left nothing to do but sit in my chair by the side of my bed and wait for breakfast. Breakfast, on a cart, was wheeled in and eaten. After breakfast we were left alone until lunch time. Then lunch would be wheeled in.

Near the door to the latrine there was a huge oak table. Spaced around the table there were shiny chromium chairs with colorful comfortable cushions that whooshed when you first sat down. Along the wall behind the table were stack after stack of old magazines. Except for the brief interruptions for meals and blood-tests I killed the entire first day by going through them. I considered it a pleasant day. I didn't have to think about anything. I didn't have to do anything, and I didn't have anything to worry about. The first night following my admittance I slept like a dead man.

The next morning, after a plain but filling breakfast of mush, buttered toast, orange juice and coffee, I proceeded to the stacks of magazines again. I had a fresh package of king-sized cigarettes furnished by the Red Cross and I was set for another pleasant day. We were not allowed to keep matches and it was inconvenient to get a light from the orderly every time I wanted to smoke, but I knew I couldn't have everything.

Digging deeply into the stacks of magazines I ran across old copies of *Art Digest, The American Artist* and *The Modern Painter.* This was a find that pleased me. It had been a long time since I had done any reading and although the magazines were old, I hadn't read any of them. One at a time I read them through, cover to cover. I skipped nothing. I read the how-to-do's, the criticism, the personality sketches and the advertisements. It all interested me. I spent considerable time studying the illustrations of the pictures in the recent one man shows, dissecting pictures in my mind and putting them together again. It was all very nice until after lunch. I was jolted into reality. Really jolted.

There was an article in *The Modern Artist* by one of my oldest teachers at the Chicago Art Institute. It wasn't an exceptional article: he was deploring at length the plight of the creative artist in America and filling in with the old standby solution—*Art must have subsidy to survive*—when I read my name in the pages flat before me. It leaped off the pages filling my eyes. Me. Harry Jordan. A would-be suicide, a resident of a free NP ward, and here was my name in a national magazine! Not that there was so much:

". . . and what caused Harry Jordan to give up painting? Jordan was an artist who could do more with orange and brown than many painters can do with a full palette . . ."

Just that much, but it was enough to dissolve my detached feelings and bring me back to a solid awareness of my true situation. My old teacher was wrong, of course. I hadn't given up painting for economic reasons. No real artist ever does. Van Gogh, Gauguin, Modigliani and a thousand others are the answer to that. But the mention of my name made me realize how far I had dropped from sight, from what I had been, and from what I might have been in my Chicago days. My depression returned full force. A nagging shred of doubt dangled in front of me. Maybe I could paint after all? Didn't my portrait of Helen prove that to me? Certainly, no painter could have captured her as well as I had done. Was I wrong? Had I wasted the years I could have been painting? Wouldn't it have been better to stay close to art, even as a teacher, where at least I would have had the urge to work from time to time? Maybe I would have overcome the block? The four early paintings I had done in orange-and-brown, the non-objective abstractions were still remembered by my old teacher—after all the elapsed time. It shook my convictions. Rocked me. My ruminations were rudely disturbed. My magazine was rudely jerked out of my hands.

"That's my magazine!" I turned in the direction of the high, reedy voice, verging on hysteria. A slight blond man stood by the table, clutching *The Modern Artist* to his pigeon breast. His face was flushed an angry red and his watery blue eyes were tortured with an inner pain.

"Sure," I said noncommittally, "I was just looking at it."

"I'll stick your arm in boiling water!" He informed me shrilly.

"No you won't." I didn't know what else to say to the man.

"I'll stick your arm in boiling water! I'll stick your arm in boiling water! I'll stick your arm in—" He kept repeating it over and over, his voice growing louder and higher, until Conrad was attracted from the end of the ward. Conrad covered the floor in quick strides, took the little man by the arm and led him away from the table.

"I want to show you something," Conrad told the man secretly.

"What are you going to show me?" The feverish face relaxed somewhat and he followed Conrad down the ward to his bed. Conrad showed him his chair and the man sat down wearily and buried his face in his hands. On the walk to his bed and chair, the magazine was forgotten, and it fell to the floor. On his way back to the table, Conrad picked up the magazine, slapped it on the table in front of me, and returned to his desk without a word of explanation. A man who had been watching the scene from the door of the latrine, crossed to the table and sat down opposite me.

"Don't worry about him," he said. "He's a schitzo."

"A what?"

"Schitzo. That's short for schizophrenic. In addition to that, he's a paranoid."

I looked the patient over carefully who was talking to me. Unlike the rest of us he wore a pair of yellow silk pajamas, and an expensive vermillion brocade robe. His face was lined with crinkly crescents about his eyes and mouth and a lightning blaze of white shot through his russet hair above each ear. He was smiling broadly; the little scene had amused him.

"My name is Mr. Haas," he told me, reaching out to shake hands.

"Harry Jordan," I said, shaking his hand.

"After a few years," he offered, "you get so you can tell. I've been in and out of these places ever since the war. I'm a Schitzo myself and also paranoid. What's the matter with you?"

"Nothing," I said defensively.

"You're lucky then. Why are your wrists bandaged?"

"I tried suicide, but it didn't work."

"You're a manic-depressive then."

"No, I'm not," I said indignantly. "I'm nothing at all."

"Don't fight it, Jordan," Mr. Haas had a kind, pleasant voice. "It's only a label. It doesn't mean anything. Take my case for instance. I tried to kill my wife this time, and she had me committed. I won't be in here long, I'm being trans-fered to a V.A. hospital, and this time for good. It isn't so bad being a Schitzo; there are many compensations. Did you ever have hallucinations?"

"No. Never."

"I have them all the time, and the best kind. Most of us hear voices, but my little hallucination comes to me in the night and I can hear him, smell him and feel him. He feels like a rubber balloon filled with warm water, and he smells like Chanel Number Five. We carry on some of the damnd-est conversations you've ever heard."

"What does he look like?" I was interested.

"The hell with you, Jordan. Get your own hallucination. How about some chess?"

"I haven't played in a long time," I said.

"Neither have I. I'll get my board and chessmen."

For the rest of the day I played chess with Mr. Haas. I didn't win a game.

By supper that night I was my old self again. Playing chess had made me forget the magazine article temporarily. After a supper of liver and new potatoes I crawled into bed. I was a failure and I knew it. The false hopes of the early afternoon were gone. The portrait of Helen was nothing but a lucky accident. My old orange-and-brown abstracts were nothing but experiments. Picasso's *Blue* period. Jordan's *Orange-and-Brown* period. They hadn't sold at my asking price and I'd destroyed them years ago. My name being mentioned, along with a dozen other painters, was no cause for emotion or elation. It was all padding. The prof. had to pad his article some way, and he had probably wracked his brain for enough names to make his point. But seeing my name in *The Modern Artist* had ruined my day.

It took me a long time to fall asleep.

The next morning I awoke with a slight headache and a sharp pain behind my eyeballs. I wasn't hungry, my hands were trembling slightly and my heart had a dull, dead ache. I felt terrible and even the hot water of the shower didn't relieve my depression.

I was back to normal.

At nine-thirty Conrad told me the doctor wanted to see me. He led the way and I sluffed along behind him in my slippers. Dr. Davidson's office was a small bare room, without a window, and lighted by fluorescent tubing the length of the ceiling. Two wooden chairs and a metal desk. The desk was stacked with patient's charts in aluminum covers. I sat down across from Dr. Davidson and Conrad closed the door, leaving us alone.

"Did you think I'd forgotten about you, Jordan?" The doctor tried a thin-lipped smile.

"No, sir." My fists were tightly clenched and I kept my eyes on my bandaged wrists.

"You forgot to fill in the forms I gave you."

"No, I didn't. I read the questions and that was enough."

"We need that information in order to admit you, Jordan."

"You won't get it from me. I'm ready to leave anyway." I got to my feet and half-way to the door.

"Sit down, Jordan." I sat down again. "What's the matter? Don't you want to tell me about it?"

"Not particularly. It all seems silly now. Although it seemed like a good idea at the time."

"Nothing is silly here," he said convincingly, "or strange, or secret. I'd like to hear about it."

"There's nothing really to tell. I was depressed, as I usually am, and I passed my depression on to Helen—Mrs. Meredith. We cut our wrists."

"But why are you depressed?"

"Because I'm a failure. I don't know how else to say it."

"How long had you been drinking?"

"Off and on. Mostly on. Helen drinks more than I do. I don't consider myself an alcoholic, but I suppose she is, or close to it."

"How long have you been drinking?"

"About five years."

"I mean you and Mrs. Meredith."

"Since we've been together. Three weeks, a month. Something like that."

"What have you used for money? Are you employed?"

"Not now. She had a couple of hundred dollars. It's gone now. That's part of this." I held up my arms. "No money."

"What kind of work do you do when you work?"

"Counterman, fry cook, dishwasher."

"Is that all?"

"I used to teach. Painting, drawing and so on. Fine arts."

"Why did you give it up?"

"I don't know."

"By that you mean you won't say."

"Take it any way you want."

"How were your carnal relations with Mrs. Meredith?"

"Carnal? That's a hell of a word to use, and it's none of your business!" I was as high-keyed and ill-strung as a Chinese musical instrument.

"Perhaps the word was unfortunate. How was your sex life, then?"

"How is any sex life? What kind of an answer do you want?"

"As a painter—you did paint, didn't you?" I nodded. "You should have a sharp notice for sensation, then. Where did it feel the best? The tip, the shaft, where?" He held his pencil poised over a sheet of yellow paper.

"I don't remember and it's none of your business!"

"You aren't making it easy for me to help you, Jordan," he said patiently.

"I don't need any help."

"You asked for help when you entered the hospital."

"That was my mistake. I don't need any help. I'm sorry I wasted your time. Just let me out and I'll be all right."

"All right, Jordan. I'll have you released in the morning."

I stood up, anxious to get away from him. "Thanks, Doctor. I'm sorry—"

"Sit down!" I sat down again. "I've already talked to Mrs. Meredith, but I wanted to check with you. Is Mrs. Meredith colored?"

"Helen?" My laugh was hard and brittle. "Of course not. What made you ask that?"

He hesitated for a moment before he answered. "Her expression and eyes, the bone structure of her face. She denied it too, but I thought I'd check with you."

"No," I said emphatically. "She definitely isn't colored."

"I'm going to tell you something, Jordan. I think you need help. As a rule, I don't give advice; people don't take it and it's a waste of time. But in your case I want to mention a thing or two. My own personal opinion. I don't think you and Mrs. Meredith are good for each other. All I can see ahead for you both is tragedy. That is, if you continue to live together."

"Thanks for your opinion. Can I go now?"

"Yes, you can go."

"Will you release Helen tomorrow too?"

"In a few more days."

"Can I see her?"

"No, I don't think so. It would be best for her not to have any visitors for the next few days."

"If you'll call Big Mike's Bar and Grill and ask for me, I'll pick her up when you release her."

"All right." He wrote the address on the sheet of yellow paper. "You can go back to your ward."

Conrad met me outside the office and took me back to the ward. For the rest of the day I played chess with Mr. Haas. I didn't win any games, but my skill improved. I couldn't sleep that night, and finally I got out of bed at eleven and asked the nurse to give me something. She gave me a sleeping pill that worked and I didn't awaken until morning. As soon as breakfast was over with my clothes were brought to me and I put them on. Mr. Haas talked with me while I was dressing.

"I'm sorry to see you leave so soon, Jordan. In another day or so you might have won a game." He laughed pleasantly. "And then I would have killed you." I didn't know whether he was kidding or not. "Makes you think, doesn't it?" he added. We shook hands and I started toward the door. "I'll be seeing you!" He called after me, and laughed again. This time rather unpleasantly, I thought. Conrad took me to the elevator and told me to stop at the desk in the lobby. At the desk downstairs, the nurse on duty gave me three pieces of paper to sign, and in a moment I was out on the street.

There wasn't any sun and the fog had closed down heavily over the city. I walked through the damp mist, up and down the hills, alone in my own little pocket of isolation. I walked slowly, but in what seemed like a short length of time I found myself in front of Big Mike's. I pushed through the swinging door, sat down at the bar and put my shaving kit on the seat beside me.

"Hello, Harry," Mike said jovially. "Where you been keeping yourself?"

"Little trip."

"Drink?"

I shook my head. "Mike, I need some money. No, I don't want a loan," I said when he reached for his hip pocket. "I want a job. Can you use me for a few days as a busboy or dishwasher?"

"I've got a dishwasher," Mike rubbed his chin thoughtfully. "But I don't have a busboy. Maybe the waiters would appreciate a man hustling dishes at noon and dinner. That's a busy time. But I can't pay you anything, Harry—dollar an hour."

"That's plenty. It would really help out while I look for a job."

"Want to start now?"

"Sure."

"Pick up a white jacket in the kitchen."

I started to work, grateful for the opportunity. The waiters were glad to have me clearing dishes and carrying them to the kitchen. I'm a fast worker and I kept the tables cleared for them all through the lunch hour, hotfooting it back and forth to the kitchen with a tray in each hand. By two-thirty the lunch crowd had slowed to a dribble and I was off until five. I took the time to go to my roominghouse for a shower. I straightened the room, dumped trash and beer bottles into the can in the backyard, returned to Mike's. I worked until ten that evening, returned to my room.

I found it was impossible to get to sleep. I quit trying to force it, dressed and went outside. I walked for a while and suddenly started to run. I ran around the block three times and was soon gasping for breath. I kept running. My heart thumped so hard I could feel it beating through my shirt. Bright stars danced in front of my eyes, turned gray, black. I had to stop. I leaned against a building, gasping until I got my breath back. My muscles twitched and ached as I slowly made my way back home. I took a shower and threw myself across the bed. Now I could sleep, and I did until ten the next morning.

It was three days before Dr. Davidson called me. It was in the middle of the noon rush and I was dripping wet when Mike called me to the telephone at the end of the bar. I didn't say anything, but held my hand over the mouthpiece until he walked away.

"Jordan here," I said into the phone.

"This is Doctor Davidson, Jordan. We've decided to release Mrs. Meredith in your custody. As her common-law husband you'll be responsible for her. Do you understand that?"

"What time?" I asked impatiently.

"About three this afternoon. You'll have to sign for her to take her out. Sure you want to do it?"

"Yes, sir. I'll be there." I racked the phone.

Big Mike was in the kitchen eating a salami sandwich and talking with the chef. The chef was complaining about the quality of the pork loin he was getting lately. I broke into the monologue.

"Mike, I have to quit."

"Okay."

"Can I have my money?"

"Okay." He took a roll of bills out of his hip pocket, peeled six ones and handed them to me.

"Only six bucks?"

"I took out for your tab, Harry, but I didn't charge your meals."

"Thanks, Mike. I don't like to leave you in the middle of a rush like this—" I began to apologize.

He waved me away impatiently, bit into his sandwich. "Forget it."

I hung the white mess jacket in the closet and slipped into my corduroy jacket. At the rooming house I showered and shaved for the second time that day. I rubbed my worn shoes with a towel but they were in such bad shape they didn't shine a bit. I caught a trolley, transferred to a bus, transferred to another trolley. It was one-thirty when I reached the entrance to the hospital. I sat down on a bench in the little park and watched the minute hand in the electric clock bounce to each mark, rarely taking my eyes away from it. The clock was set into the center of a Coca-Cola sign above the door of a drug store in the shopping center across the street. At three, on the head, I entered the hospital lobby. Helen was waiting for me by the circular counter, her lower lip quivering. As soon as she saw me she began to cry. I held her tight and kissed her, to the annoyance of the nurse.

"Hey," I said softly. "Cut that out. Everything's going to be all right." Her crying stopped as suddenly as it started. I signed the papers the nurse had ready, picked up Helen's bag and we went outside. We sat down on the bench in the little park.

"How'd they treat you, sweetheart?" I asked her.

"Terrible." Helen shuddered. "Simply terrible, and it was boring as hell."

"What did Dr. Davidson say to you? Anything?"

"He said I should quit drinking. That's about all."

"Anything else?"

"A lot of personal questions. He's got a filthy mind."

"Are you going to quit drinking?"

"Why should I? For him? That bastard!"

"Do you want a drink now?"

"It's all I've thought about all week, Harry," she said sincerely.

"Come on," I took her arm, helping her to her feet. "Let's go across the street."

A few doors down the street from the shopping center we found a small neighborhood bar. We entered and sat down in the last booth. I saved out enough money for carfare and we drank the rest of the six dollars. Helen was unusually quiet and drank nothing but straight shots, holding the glass in both hands, like a child holding a mug. Once in awhile she would almost cry, and then she would smile instead. We didn't talk; there was nothing to talk about. We left the bar and made the long, wearisome trip back to Big Mike's. We sat down in our old seats at the bar and started to drink on a new tab. Mike was glad to see Helen again and he saw that we always had a fresh, full glass in front of us. By midnight Helen was glassy-eyed drunk and I took her home and put her to bed. Despite the many drinks I had had, I was comparatively sober. Before going to bed myself I smoked a cigarette, crushed it savagely in the ashtray.

As far as I could tell, we were no better off than before.

mother love

Next morning I got out of bed early, and without waking Helen, took a long hot shower and dressed. Helen slept soundly, her lips slightly parted. I raised the blind and the room flooded with bright sunlight. A beautiful day. I shook Helen gently by the shoulder and she opened her eyes quickly, blinked them against the brightness. She was wide awake.

"I hated to wake you out of a sound sleep." I said, "but I'm leaving."

Helen sat up in bed immediately. "Leaving? Where?"

"Job hunting." I grinned at her alarm. "Not a drop of whiskey in the house."

"No money at all, huh?"

"No money, no coffee, nothing at all."

"What time will you be back?"

"I don't know. Depends on whether I can get a job, and if I do, when I get through. But I'll be back as soon as I can."

Helen got out of bed, slid her arms around my neck and kissed me hard on the mouth. "You shouldn't have to work, Harry," she said sincerely and impractically. "You shouldn't have to do anything except paint."

"Yeah," I said, disengaging her arms from my neck, "and make love to you. I'd better get going." I left the room, closing the door behind me.

There was a little change in my pocket, more than enough for carfare, and I caught the cable car downtown to Market Street. I had always been lucky finding jobs on Market, maybe I could again. There are a thousand and one cafes. One of them needed a man like me. From Turk Street I walked toward the Civic Center, looking for signs in windows. I wasn't particular. Waiter, dishwasher, anything, I didn't care. I tried two cafes without success. At last I saw a sign: FRY COOK WANTED, hanging against the inside of a window, of a small cafe, attached with scotch tape. I entered the cafe. It was a dark, dingy place with an overpowering smell of fried onions. I reached over the shoulder of the peroxide blonde sitting behind the cash register and jerked the sign out of the window.

"What do you think you're doing?" she said indifferently.

"I'm the new fry cook. Where's the boss?"

"In the kitchen." She jerked her thumb toward the rear of the cafe, appraising me with blue, vacant eyes.

I made my way toward the kitchen. The counter was filled, all twelve stools, and the majority of the customers sitting on them were waiting for their food. There wasn't even a counterman working to give a glass of water or pass out a menu. The boss, a perspiring, overweight Italian, wearing suit pants and a white shirt, was gingerly dishing chile beans into a bowl. Except for the old, slow-moving dishwasher, he was the only one in the kitchen.

"Need a fry cook?" I grinned ingratiatingly, holding up the sign.

"Need one? You from the Alliance?"

"No, but I'm a fry cook."

"I been trying to get a cook from the Alliance for two days, and my waitress quit twenty minutes ago. The hell with the Alliance. Get busy."

"I'm your man." I removed my coat and hung it on a nail.

He wore a greasy, happy smile. "Sixty-five a week, meals and laundry."

"You don't have to convince me," I told him, "I'm working."

I wrapped an apron around my waist and took a look at the stove. The boss left the kitchen, rubbing his hands together, and started to take the orders. Although I was busy I could handle things easily enough. I can take four or five orders in my head and have four or more working on the stove at the same time. When I try to go over that I sometimes run into trouble. But there was nothing elaborate to prepare. The menu offered nothing but plain food, nothing complicated. The boss was well pleased with my work. I could tell that by the way he smiled at me when he barked in his orders. And I had taken him out of a hole.

At one my relief cook came on duty, a fellow by the name of Tiny Sanders. I told him what was working and he nodded his head and started to break eggs for a Denver with one hand. I put my jacket on, found a brown paper sack and filled it with food out of the icebox. I don't believe in buying food when I'm working in a cafe. The boss came into the kitchen and I hit him up for a five spot. He opened his wallet and gave me the five without hesitation.

"I'm giving you the morning shift, Jordan. Five a.m. to one."

"That's the shift I want." I told him. "See you in the morning." It was the best shift to have. It would give me every afternoon and evening with Helen.

I left the cafe and on the corner I bought a dozen red carnations for a dollar from a sidewalk vendor. They were old flowers and I knew they wouldn't last for twenty-four hours, but they would brighten up our room. On the long ride home I sniffed the fragrance of the carnations and felt well-pleased with myself, revelling in my good fortune.

I was humming to myself as I ran up the stairs and down the hall to our room.

I opened my door and jagged tendrils of perfume clawed at my nostrils. Tweed. It was good perfume, but there was too much of a good thing. Helen, fully dressed in her best suit, was sitting nervously on the edge of the unmade bed. Across from her in the strongest chair was a formidable woman in her late fifties. Her hair was a streaked slate-gray and she was at least fifty pounds overweight for her height—about five-nine. Her sharp blue eyes examined me like a bug through a pair of eight-sided gold-rimmed glasses. The glasses were on a thin gold chain that led to a shiny black button pinned to the breast of a rather severe blue taffeta dress.

"Harry," there was a catch in Helen's throat, "this is my mother, Mrs. Mathews."

"How do you do?" I said. I put the carnations and sack of food on the table. "This is a pleasant surprise."

"Is it?" Mrs. Mathews sniffed.

"Well, I didn't expect you—"

"I'll bet you didn't!" She jerked her head to the right. "The hospital notified Mother I was ill," Helen explained.

"That was very thoughtful of them," I said.

"Yes," Mrs. Mathews said sarcastically, "wasn't it? Yes, it was very thoughtful indeed. They also were thoughtful enough to inform me that my daughter was released from the hospital in the custody of her common-law husband. That was a nice pleasant surprise!"

For a full minute there was a strained silence. I interrupted it. "Helen is all right now," I said, trying a cheery note.

"Is she?" Mrs. Mathews asked.

"Yes, she is."

"Well, I don't think so," Mrs. Mathews jerked her head to the right. "I think she's out of her mind!"

"Please, Mother!" Helen was very close to tears.

"I'm taking good care of Helen," I said.

"Are you?" Mrs. Mathews hefted herself to her feet, clomped heavily across the room to the portrait. "Is this what you call taking good care of her? Forcing her to pose for a filthy, obscene picture?" Her words were like vitriolic drops of acid wrapped in cellophane, and they fell apart when they left her lips, filling the room with poison.

"It's only a portrait," I said defensively. "It isn't for public viewing."

"You bet it isn't! Only a depraved mind could have conceived it; only a depraved beast could execute it; and only a leering, concupiscant goat would look at it."

"You're too hard on me, Mrs. Mathews. It isn't that bad," I said.

"Where have you been so long, Harry?" Helen asked me, trying to change the subject.

"I got a job, and that sack's full of groceries," I said, pointing.

"What kind of a job?" Mrs. Mathews asked. "Sweeping streets?"

"No. I'm a cook."

"I don't doubt it. Listen, er, ah, Mr. Jordan, if you think anything of Helen at all you'll talk some sense into her. I want her to come home with me, where she belongs. Look at her eyes! They look terrible."

"Now that I've got a job she'll be all right, Mrs. Mathews. Would you like a salami sandwich, Helen?"

"No thanks, Harry," Helen said politely. "Not right now."

"Why not?" Mrs. Mathews asked with mock surprise. "That's exactly what you should eat! Not fresh eggs, milk, orange juice and fruit. That stuff isn't any good for a person right out of a sick bed. Go ahead. Eat a salami sandwich. With pickles!"

"I'm not hungry, Mother!"

"Maybe it's a drink of whiskey you want? Have you got whiskey in that sack, Mr. Jordan, or is it all salami?"

"Just food," I said truthfully. "No whiskey."

"That's something. Are you aware that Helen shouldn't drink anything with alcohol in it? Do you know of her bad heart? Did she tell you she was sick in bed with rheumatic fever for three years when she was a little girl? Did she tell you she couldn't smoke?"

"I'm all right, Mother!" Helen said angrily. "Leave Harry alone!"

Again we suffered a full minute of silence. "I brought you some carnations," I said to Helen; "you'd better put them in water." I crossed to the table, unwrapped the green paper, and gave the flowers to Helen.

"They're lovely, Harry!" Helen exclaimed. She placed the carnations in the water pitcher on the dresser, arranged them quickly, inexpertly, sat down again on the edge of the bed, and stared at her mother. I sat beside her, reached over and took her hand. It was warm, almost feverish.

"Now listen to me, both of you." Mrs. Mathews spoke slowly, as though she were addressing a pair of idiots. "I can perceive that neither one of you has got enough sense to come in out of the rain. Helen has, evidently, made up what little mind she has, to remain under your roof instead of mine. All right. She's over twenty-one and there's nothing I can do about it. If you don't dissuade her and I can see you won't—not that I blame you—will you at least let me in on your plans?"

"We're going to be married soon." Helen said.

"Do you mind if I call to your attention that you're already married?" Mrs. Mathews jerked her head to the right as though Helen's husband was standing outside the door waiting for her.

"I mean, after I get a divorce," Helen said.

"And meanwhile, while you're waiting, you intend to continue to live here in sin? Is that right?"

Helen didn't answer for a moment and I held my breath. "Yes, Mother, that's what I'm going to do. Only it isn't sin."

"I won't quibble." Mrs. Mathews sniffed, jerked her head to the right and turned her cold blue eyes on me. "How much money do you make per week, Mr. Jordan? Now that you have a job." The way she said it, I don't believe she thought I had a job.

"Sixty-five dollars a week. And I get my meals and laundry."

"That isn't enough. And I doubt in here—" she touched her mammoth left breast with her hand— "whether you can hold a position paying that much for any length of time. Here's what I intend to do. As long as my daughter won't listen to reason, I'll send her a check for twenty-five dollars a week. But under one condition: both of you, stay out of San Sienna!"

"We don't need any money from you, Mother!" Helen said fiercely. "Harry makes more than enough to support me."

"I'm not concerned with that," Mrs. Mathews said self-righteously. "I know where my duty lies. You can save the money if you don't need it, or tear up the check, I don't care. But starting right now, I'm giving you twenty-five dollars a week!"

"You're very generous," I said.

"I'm not doing it for you," Mrs. Mathews jerked her head to the right. "I'm doing it for Helen."

Mrs. Mathews removed a checkbook and ballpoint pen from the depths of a cavernous saddle-leather bag and wrote a check. She crossed the room to the dresser, drying the ink by waving the check in the air, and put the filled-in check beside the pitcher of carnations. She sniffed.

"That's all I have to say, but to repeat it one more time so there'll be no mistake: Stay out of San Sienna!"

"It was nice meeting you, Mrs. Mathews," I said. Helen remained silent.

Mrs. Mathews jerked her head to the right so hard her glasses were pulled off her nose. The little chain spring caught them up and they whirred up to the black button pinned to her dress. She closed the shirred beaver over the glasses, sniffed, and slammed the door in my face.

But the memory lingered on, in the form of a cloud of Tweed perfume.

Helen's face was pale and her upper lip was beaded with tiny drops of perspiration. She wound her arms round my waist tightly and pressed her face into my chest. I patted her on the back, kissed the top of her head.

"Oh, Harry, it was terrible!" Her voice was low and muffled against my chest. "She's been here since ten o'clock this morning. Arguing, arguing, arguing! Trying to break me down. And I almost lost! I was within that much"—she pulled away from me, held thumb and forefinger an inch apart—"of going with her." She looked at me accusingly; her face wore an almost pitiful expression. "Where were you? When I needed you the most, you weren't here!"

"I wasn't lying about the job, Helen. I found a job as a fry cook and had to go to work to get it."

"Why do you have to work? It isn't fair to leave me here all alone."

"We have to have money, sweetheart," I explained

patiently. "We were flat broke when I went out this morning, if you remember."

"Can't we live on what money Mother sends us?"

"We could barely exist on twenty-five dollars a week. The room rent's ten dollars, and we'd have to buy food and liquor out of the rest. We just can't do it."

"What are we going to do, Harry? It's so unfair of Mother!" she said angrily. "She could just as easily give us two hundred and fifty a week!"

"Can't you see what she's up to, Helen? She's got it all planned out, she thinks. She doesn't want you to go hungry, but if she gave us more money, she knows damned well you'd never go back to her. This way, she figures she has a chance—"

"Well, she's wrong! I'm never going back to San Sienna!"

"That leaves it up to me then, where it belongs. I'll work this week out, anyway. Maybe another. We'll pay some room rent in advance that way, and the tab at Mike's. And maybe we can get a few loose dollars ahead. Then I'll look for some kind of part time work that'll give me more time with you."

We left it at that.

Helen picked the check up from the dresser and left for the delicatessen. She returned in a few minutes with a bottle of whiskey and a six-pack carton of canned beer. I had one drink with her and I made it last. I didn't want to drink that one. I felt that the situation was getting to be too much for me to handle. Helen drank steadily, pouring them down, one after the other, chasing the raw whiskey with sips of beer. Her mother's visit had upset her badly, and she faced it typically, the way she faced every situation.

By six that evening she sat numbly in the chair by the window. She was in a paralyzed stupor. I undressed her and put her to bed. She lay on her back, breathing with difficulty. Her eyes were like dark bruises, her face a mask of fragile, white tissue paper.

I didn't leave the room; I felt like a sentry standing guard duty. I made a salami sandwich, took one bite, and threw it down on the table. I sat in the chair staring at the wall until well past midnight.

After I went to bed, it was a long time before I fell asleep.

bottle baby 11

The little built-in, automatic alarm clock inside my head waked me at four a.m. and I hadn't even taken the trouble to set it. I tried to fight against it and go back to sleep, but I couldn't. The alarm was too persistent. I reluctantly got out of the warm bed, shiveringly grabbed a towel, and rushed next door to the bathroom. Standing beneath the hot water of the shower almost put me back to sleep. With an involuntary yelp I twisted the faucet to cold and remained under the pelting needles of ice for three minutes. On the way back to my room I dried myself, and then dressed hurriedly against the background of my chattering teeth. The room was much too cold to hang around for coffee to boil and I decided to wait and get a cup when I reached Vitale's Cafe. I got my trenchcoat out of the closet and put it on over my corduroy jacket. The trenchcoat was so filthy dirty I only wore it when I had to, but it was so cold inside the house I knew I would freeze on the street without something to break the wind.

Helen was sleeping on her side facing the wall and I couldn't see her face. Her hip made a minor mountain out of the covers and a long ski slope down to her bare round shoulder. I envied Helen's warmness but I pulled the blanket up a little higher and tucked it in all around her neck.

Helen had been so far under the night before when I put her to bed I thought it best to leave a note. I tore a strip of paper from the top of a brown sack and wrote in charcoal:

> Dearest Angel,
> Your slave has departed for the salt mine. Will be home by
> one-thirty at latest. All my love,
>   Harry

Helen's bottle of whiskey was still a quarter full. I put the note in the center of the table and weighted it with the bottle where I knew she would find it easily when she first got out of bed. I turned out the overhead light and closed the door softly on my way out.

It was colder outside than I had anticipated it to be. A strong, steady wind huffed in from the bay, loaded-heavily with salt and mist, and I couldn't make myself stand still on the corner to wait for my car. Cable cars are few and far between at four-twenty in the morning and it was far warmer to run a block, wait, run a block and wait until one came into view. I covered four blocks this way and the exertion warmed me enough to wait on the fourth corner until a car came along and slowed down enough for me to catch it. I paid my fare to the conductor and went inside. I was the only passenger for several blocks and then business picked up for the cable car when several hungry-looking longshoremen boarded it with neatly-lettered placards on their way to the docks to picket. I dismounted at the Powell Street turnaround and walked briskly down Market with my hands shoved deep in my pockets. The wide street was as nearly deserted as it can ever be. There were a few early-cruising cabs and some middle-aged paper boys on the corners waiting for the first morning editions. There was an ugly mechanical monster hugging the curbs and sploshing water and brushing it up behind as it noisily cleaned at the streets. Later on there would be the regular street cleaners with brooms and trash-cans on wheels to pick up what the monster missed. I entered Vitale's Cafe.

"Morning, Mr. Vitale," I said.

"It don't work for me," the boss said ruefully. "I poured hot water through ten times already and it won't turn dark. I have to use fresh coffee grounds after all."

"Did you dry the old grounds on the stove first?"

"No, I been adding hot water."

"That's what's the matter then. If you want to use coffee grounds two days in a row you have to dry them out on the stove in a shallow pan. Add a couple of handfuls of fresh coffee to the dried grounds and the coffee'll be as dark as cheap coffee ever gets."

I took off my jacket and lit the stove and checked on the groceries for breakfast. I wrapped an apron around my waist and stoned the grill while I waited for the coffee to be made, making a mental note to fix my own coffee the next morning before I left my room. By five a.m. I was ready for work and nobody had entered the cafe. I wondered why Vitale opened so early. I soon found out. All of a sudden the counter was jammed with breakfast eaters from the various office buildings and street, most of them ordering the Open Eye Breakfast Special: two ounces of tomato juice, one egg, one strip of bacon, one piece of toast and coffee extra. This breakfast was served for thirty-five cents and although it was meager fare it attracted the low income group. The night elevator operators, the cleaning women, the news-boys, the all-night movie crowd, and some of the police-men going off duty all seemed to go for it. Breakfast was served all day at Vitale's, but at ten-thirty I checked the pale blue menu and began to get ready for the lunch crowd. I was so busy during the noon rush I hated to look up from my fry grill when Tiny, my relief, tapped me on the shoul-der at one on the head. I told Tiny what was working, wrapped up two one-pound T-bones to take home with me, and left the cafe with a wave at the boss.

On the long ride home I tried to think of ways to bring Helen out of the doldrums, but every idea I thought of was an idea calling for money. By the time I reached my corner my immediate conclusion was that all Helen needed was one of my T-bone steaks, fried medium rare as only I could fry a steak and topped with a pile of french fried onion rings. I bought a dime's worth of onions at the delicatassen and hurried home with my surprise. I opened the door to my room and Helen wasn't there. My note was still under the whiskey bottle, but now the bottle was empty. There was a message from Helen written under mine and I picked it up and studied it.

> *Dear Harry,*
> *I can't sit here all day waiting for you. If I don't talk to somebody I'll go nuts. I love you.*
> *Helen*

The message was in Helen's unmistakable microscopic handwriting and it was written with the same piece of charcoal I had used and left on the table. It took me several minutes to decipher what she said and I still didn't know what she really meant. Was she leaving me for good? I opened the closet and checked her clothes, the few she had. They were all in the closet and so was her suitcase. That made me feel a little better, knowing she wasn't leaving me. I still didn't like the idea of her running around loose, half-drunk, and with nothing solid in her stomach. She had killed the rest of the whiskey, which was more than a half-pint, and she had the remainder of the twenty-five bucks her mother had given her. She could be anywhere in San Francisco—with anybody. I had to find her before she got into trouble.

I opened the window, put the steaks outside on the sill, and closed the window again. If the sun didn't break through the fog they would keep until that evening before they spoiled. I left the rooming house and walked down the street to Big Mike's Bar and Grill. After I entered the grill I made my way directly to the cash register where Big Mike was standing. By the look in his eyes I could tell he didn't want to talk to me.

"Have you seen Helen, Mike?" I asked him.

"Yeah, I saw her all right. She was in here earlier."

"She left, huh?"

"That's right, Harry. She left." His voice was surly, his expression sour. There was no use to question him any further. How was he supposed to know where she went? It was obvious something was bothering him and I waited for him to tell me about it.

"Listen, Harry," Mike said, after I waited a full minute. "I like you fine, and I suppose Helen's okay too, but from now on I don't want her in here when you ain't with her."

"What happened, Mike. I've been working since five this morning."

"I don't like to say nothing, Harry, but, you might as well know. She was in about eleven and drunker than hell. I wouldn't sell her another drink even, and when I won't sell another drink, they're drunk. She had her load on when she came in, and it was plenty. Anyway, she got nasty with me and I told her to leave. She wouldn't go and I didn't want to toss her out on her ear so I shoved her in a booth and had Tommy take her some coffee. She poured it on the floor, cussing Tommy out and after awhile three Marines took up with her. They sat down in her booth and she quieted down so I let it go. After a while they all left and that was it. I'm sorry as hell, Harry, but that's the way it was. I ain't got time to look after every drunk comes in here."

"I know it, Mike. You don't know where they went, do you?"

"As I said, after a while I looked and they were gone."

"Well, thanks, Mike." I left the bar and went out on the sidewalk. If the Marines and Helen had taken the cable car downtown I'd never find them. But if they took a cab from the hack-stand in the middle of the block, maybe I would be all right. I turned toward the hack-stand. Bud, the young Korean veteran driver for the Vet's Cab Company was leaning against a telephone pole waiting for his phone to ring, a cigarette glued to the corner of his mouth, when I reached his stand. He had a pinched, fresh face with light beige-colored eyes, and wore his chauffeur's cap so far back on his head it looked like it would fall off. I knew him enough to nod to him, and saw him often around the corner and in Big Mike's, but I had never spoken to him before.

"I guess you're lookin' for your wife, huh, Jordan?" Bud made a flat statement and it seemed to give him great satisfaction.

"Yes, I am, Bud. Have you seen her?"

"Sure did." He ripped the cigarette out of his mouth, leaving a powdering of flaked white paper on his lower lip, and snapped the butt into the street. "She was with three Marines." This statement gave him greater satisfaction.

"Did you take them any place?"

"Sure did."

"Where?"

"Get in." Bud opened the back door of his cab.

"What's the tariff, Bud?" I was thinking of the three one dollar bills in my watch pocket and my small jingle of change.

"It'll run you about a buck and a half." He smiled with the left side of his face. "If you want to go. She was with three Marines." He held up three fingers. "Three," he repeated, "and you are one." He held up one finger. "One."

"We'll see," I said noncommittally and climbed into the back seat.

Bud drove me to The Green Lobster, a bar and grill near Fisherman's Wharf. The bar was too far away from the Wharf for the heavy tourist trade, but it was close enough to catch the overflow on busy days and there was enough fish stink in the air to provide an atmosphere for those who felt they needed it. On the way, Bud gave me a sucker ride in order to run up his buck and a half on the meter. At most the fare should have been six-bits, but I didn't complain. I rode the unnecessary blocks out of the way and paid the fare in full when he stopped at The Green Lobster.

"This is where I left 'em," he said. I waited on the curb until he pulled away. I couldn't understand Bud's attitude. He might have been a friend of the guy I had a fight with in Big Mike's or he might have resented me having a beautiful girl like Helen. I didn't know, but I resented his manner. I like everybody and it's always disconcerting when someone doesn't like me. I entered The Green Lobster and sat down at the end of the bar near the door.

A long, narrow bar hugged the right side of the room for the full length of the dimly lighted room. There were high, wrinkled red-leather stools for the patrons and I perched on one, my feet on the chromium rungs. The left wall had a row of green-curtained booths, and between the booths and the narrow bar, there were many small tables for two covering the rest of the floorspace. Each small table was covered with a green oilcloth cover and held a bud vase with an unidentifiable artificial flower. I surveyed the room in the bar mirror and spotted Helen and the three Marines in the second booth. The four of them leaned across their table their heads together, and then they sat back and laughed boisterously. I couldn't hear them but supposed they were taking turns telling dirty jokes. Helen's laugh was loud, clear, and carried across the room above the laughter of the Marines. I hadn't heard her laugh like that since the night I first brought her home with me. After the bartender finished with two other customers at the bar he got around to me.

"Straight shot," I told him.

"It's a dollar a shot," he said quietly, half-apologetically.

"I've got a dollar," and I fished one out of my watch pocket and slapped it on the bar.

He set an empty glass before me and filled it to the brim with bar whiskey. I sipped a little off the top, put the glass back down on the bar. At a dollar a clip the shot would have to last me. I didn't have a plan or course of action, so I sat stupidly, watching Helen and the Marines in the bar mirror, trying to think of what to do next.

If I tried a direct approach and merely asked Helen to leave with me, there would be a little trouble. Not knowing what to do, I did nothing. There was one sergeant and two corporals, all three of them bigger than me. They wore neat, bright-blue Marine uniforms and all had the fresh, well-scrubbed look that servicemen have on the first few hours of leave or pass. But in my mind I didn't see them in uniform. I saw them naked, Helen naked, and all of them cavorting obscenely in a hotel room somewhere, and as this picture formed in my mind my face began to perspire.

Helen inadvertantly settled the action for me. She was in the seat against the wall, the seargant on the outside, with the two corporals facing them across the table. After a while, Helen started out of the booth to go to the ladies' room. The sergeant goosed her as she squeezed by him and she squealed, giggled, and broke clear of the table. As she looked drunkenly around the room for the door to the ladies' room she saw me sitting at the bar.

"Harry!" She screamed joyfully across the room. "Come on over!"

I half-faced her, remaining on my stool, shaking my head. Helen crossed to the bar, weaving recklessly between the tables, and as soon as she reached me, threw her arms around my neck and kissed me wetly on the mouth. The action was swift and blurred from that moment on. An attack of Marines landed on me and I was hit a glancing blow on the jaw, my right arm was twisted cruelly behind my back, and in less than a minute I was next door on the asphalt of the parking lot. A corporal held my arms behind me and another was rounding the building. The sergeant, his white belt wrapped around his fist, the buckle dangling free, waved the man back. "Go back inside, Adams, and watch that bitch! We'll take care of this bastard. She might try and get away and I spent eight bucks on her already." The oncoming corporal nodded grimly and reentered the bar. Under the circumstances I tried to be as calm as possible.

"Before you hit me with that buckle, Sergeant," I said, "why don't you let me explain?"

Businesslike, the sergeant motioned the Marine holding my arms behind my back to stand clear, so he could get a good swing at me with the belt.

"You don't have to hold me," I said over my shoulder. "If you want to beat up a man for kissing his wife, go ahead!" I jerked away and dropped to my knees in front of the sergeant. Hopefully, I prayed loudly, trying to make my voice sound sincere:

"Oh, God above! Let no man tear asunder what You have joined in holy matrimony! Dear sweet God! Deliver this poor sinner from evil, and show these young Christian gentlemen the light of Your love and Your mercy! Sweet Son of the Holy Cross and—" That was as far as I got.

"Are you and her really married?" the sergeant asked gruffly.

"Yes, sir," I said humbly, remaining on my knees and staring intently at my steepled fingers.

I glanced at the two Marines out of the corner of my eye. The youngest had a disgusted expression on his face, and was tugging at the sergeant's arm.

"Let it go, Sarge," he said, "we were took and the hell with it. I wouldn't get any fun out of hitting him now."

"Neither would I." The sergeant unwrapped the belt from his hand and buckled it around his waist. "I'm not even mad any more." There was a faint gleam of pity in his eyes as he looked at me. "If she's your wife, how come you let her run loose in the bars?"

"I was working, sir," I said, "and I thought she was home with the children." I hung my head lower, kept my eyes on the ground.

"Then it's your tough luck," the sergeant finished grimly. "Both of you got what you deserved." They left the parking lot and reentered the bar. I got off my knees, walked to the curb and waited. The sergeant brought Helen to the door, opened it for her politely, guided her outside, and as he released her arm, he cuffed her roughly across the face. Bright red marks leaped to the surface of her cheek and she reeled across the sidewalk. I caught her under the arms before she fell.

"That evens us up for the eight bucks." The sergeant grinned and shut the door.

Helen spluttered and cursed and then her body went limp in my arms. I lifted her sagging body and carried her down to the corner and the hack-stand. She hadn't really passed out; she was pretending so she wouldn't have to talk to me. I put her into the cab without help from the driver and gave him my address. I paid the eighty-cent fare when he reached my house, and hoped he didn't see the large, wet spot on the back seat until after he pulled away. Helen leaned weakly against me and I half carried her into our room and undressed her. She fell asleep immediately. Looking inside her purse, I found ninety cents in change. No bills.

I thought things over and came to a decision. I couldn't work any more and leave her by herself. Either I'd have to get money from some other source, or do without it. Left to herself, all alone, Helen would only get into serious trouble. Already I noticed things about her that had changed. She let her hair go uncombed. She skipped wearing her stockings. Her voice was slightly louder and she seemed to be getting deaf in one ear.

We never made love any more.

the dregs 12

I didn't sleep all night. I sat in the chair by the dark window with the lights out while Helen slept. I didn't try to think about anything, but kept my mind as blank as possible. When I did have a thought it was disquieting and ugly and I would get rid of it by pushing it to the back of my mind like a pack rat trading a rock for a gold nugget.

Vitale would be stuck again for a fry cook when I didn't

show up, but it couldn't be helped. To leave Helen to her own devices would be foolish. When I thought about how close I came to losing her my heart would hesitate, skip like a rock on water and then beat faster than ever. I had a day's pay coming from Vitale that I would never collect. It would take more nerve than I possessed to ask him for it. I decided to let it go.

The night passed, somehow, and as soon as the gray light hit the window I left the room and walked down the block to the delicatessen. It wasn't quite six and I had to wait for almost ten minutes before Mr. Watson opened up. I had enough money with some left over for a half-pint of whiskey and Mr. Watson pursed his lips when he put it in a sack for me.

"Most of my customers this early buy milk and eggs, Harry," he said.

"Breakfast is breakfast." I said lightly and the bells above the door tinkled as I closed it behind me.

When I got back to the room, I brought the T-bone inside from the window sill, opened the package and smelled them. They seemed to be all right and I lit the burner and dropped one in the frying pan and sprinkled it with salt. I made coffee on the other burner and watched the steak for the exact moment to turn it. To fry a steak properly it should only be turned one time. Helen awoke after awhile, got out of bed without a word or a glance in my direction and went to the bathroom. The steak was ready when she got back and I had it on a plate at the table.

"How'd you like a nice T-bone for breakfast?" I asked her.

"Ugh!" She put her feet into slippers and wrapped a flowered robe around her shoulders. "I'll settle for coffee."

I poured two cups of coffee and Helen joined me at the table. I shoved the half-pint across the table and she poured a quarter of the bottle into her coffee. I started in on the steak. We both carefully avoided any reference to the Marines or the afternoon before.

"This a day off, Harry?" Helen asked after she downed half of her laced coffee.

"No. I quit."

"Good."

"But I'm a little worried."

"What about?" She asked cautiously.

"Damned near everything. Money, for one thing, and I'm worried about you, too."

"I'm all right."

"You're drinking more than you did before, and you aren't eating."

"I'm not hungry."

"Even so, you've got to eat."

"I'm not hungry."

"Suppose . . ." I spoke slowly, choosing my words with care, "all of a sudden, just like that," and I snapped my fingers, "we quit drinking? I can pour what's left of that little bottle down the drain and we can start from there. We make a resolution and stick to it, see, stay sober from now on, make a fresh start."

Helen quickly poured another shot into her coffee. "No, Harry. I know what you mean, but I couldn't quit if I wanted to."

"Why not? We aren't getting any place the way we're going."

"Who wants to get any place?" She said sardonically. "Do you? What great pinnacle have you set your eyes on?" She rubbed her cheek gently. It was swollen from the slap the Marine had given her.

"It was just an idea." Helen was right and I was wrong. We were too far down the ladder to climb up now. I was letting my worry about money and Helen lead me into dangerous thinking. The only thing to do was keep the same level without going down any further. If I could do that, we would be all right. "Pass me the bottle," I said.

I took a good swig and I felt better immediately. From now on I wouldn't let worry get me down. I would take things as they came and with any luck at all everything would be all right.

It didn't take much to mellow Helen. After two laced cups of coffee she was feeling the drinks and listening with intent interest to my story about Van Gogh and Gauguin and their partnership at Arles. Fingernails scratched at the door. Irritated by the interruption I jerked the door open. Mrs. McQuade stood in the doorway with a large package in her arms.

"This package came for you, Mrs. Jordan," she said, looking around me at Helen. "I signed for it. It was delivered by American Express."

"Thanks, Mrs. McQuade," I said. "I'll take it." I took the package.

"That's all right. I—" She wanted to talk some more but I closed the door with my shoulder and tossed the package on the bed. Helen untied the package and opened it. It was full of women's clothing.

"It's from Mother," she said happily, "she's sent me some of my things."

"That's fine," I said. Helen started through the package, holding up various items of clothing to show me how they looked. This didn't satisfy her, and she slipped a dress on to show me how well it looked on her, removed it and started to put another one on. I was bored. But this preoccupation with a fresh wardrobe would occupy her for quite a while. Long enough for me to look around town for a way to make a few dollars. The half-pint was almost empty.

"Look, sweetheart," I said, "why don't you take your time and go through these things, and I'll go out for a while and look for a part-time job."

"But I want to show them to you—"

"And I've got to pick up a few bucks or we'll be all out of whiskey."

"Oh. How long will you be gone?"

"Not long. An hour or so at the most." I kissed her good-bye and left the house. I caught the cable car downtown and got off at Polk Street. There wasn't any particular plan or idea in my mind and I walked aimlessly down the street. I passed the Continental Garage. It was a five-story building designed solely for the parking of automobiles. At the back of the building I could see two latticed elevators that took the cars up and down to the rest of the building. On impulse, I entered the side office. There were three men in white overalls sitting around on top of the desks. They stopped talking when I entered and I smiled at the man who had MANAGER embroidered in red above the left breast pocket of his spotless overalls. He was a peppery little man with a small red moustache clipped close to his lip.

He looked at me for a moment, then closed his eyes. His eyelids were as freckled as the rest of his face.

"What I'm looking for, sir," I said, "is a part-time job. Do you have a rush period from about four to six when you could use another man to park cars?"

He opened his eyes and there was suspicion in them. "Yes and No. How come you aren't looking for an eight-hour day?"

"I am." I smiled. "I'm expecting an overseas job in Iraq," I lied. "It should come through any day now and I have to hang around the union hall all day. That's why I can't take anything permanent. But the job I'm expecting is taking a lot longer to come through than I expected and I'm running short on cash."

"I see." He nodded, compressed his lips. "You a mechanic?"

"No, sir. Petroleum engineer."

"College man, huh?" I nodded, but I didn't say anything. "Can you drive a car?"

I laughed politely. "Of course I can."

"Okay, I'll help you out. You can start this evening from four to six, parking and bringing them down. Buck and a half an hour. Take it or leave it. It's all the same to me."

"I'll take it," I said gratefully, "and thanks."

"Pete," the manager said to a loosed-jointed man with big knobby hands, "show him how to run the elevator and tell him about the tickets."

Pete left the office for the elevators and I followed him. A push button worked the elevator, but parking the cars was more complicated. The tickets were stamped with a time-stamp and parked in time groups in accordance with time of entry. When the patron brought in his stub, it was checked for the time it was brought in and the serial number of the ticket. Cars brought in early to stay all day were on the top floor and so on down to the main floor. Patrons who said they would only be gone an hour or so had their cars parked downstairs on the main floor. Five minutes after I left Pete I was on the cable car and on my way home. The fears I had in the morning were gone and I was elated. By a lucky break my part time job was solved. With the twenty-five a week coming in from Helen's mother, plus another three dollars a day from the garage, we should be able to get along fine. And counting the half-hour each way to downtown and my two hours of work, Helen would only be alone three hours.

I opened the door to our room and Helen was back in bed fast asleep. Her new clothes were scattered and thrown about the floor. Without waking her I picked them up and hung them in the closet. I wanted a shot but the little half-pint bottle was empty. I pulled the covers over Helen and lay down beside her on top of the bed. I napped fitfully till three and then I left. I started to wake her before I left, but she was sleeping so peacefully I didn't have the heart to do it.

Right after four the rush started and I hustled the cars out until six. It wasn't difficult and after a few minutes I could find the cars easily. I looked up the red-haired manager at six and he gave me three dollars and I left the garage. Going down the hallway I spread the three dollars like a fan before I opened the door to our room.

Helen was gone.

There wasn't any note so I assumed she was at Big Mike's. She had probably forgotten about the ruckus with him the day before and he was the logical man to give her a free drink, or let her sign for one. I left the roominghouse for Big Mike's. He hadn't seen her.

"If you haven't found her by now," he said, "you might as well forget about it, Harry."

"I did find her yesterday, Mike, I was with her till three this afternoon, and then I had to go to work."

"This isn't the only bar in the neighborhood." He grinned. "I wisht it was."

I made the rounds of all the neighborhood bars. She wasn't in any of them and I didn't ask any of the bartenders if she had been in them. I didn't know any of the bartenders that well. At eight-thirty I went back to the roominghouse and checked to see whether she had returned. I didn't want to miss her in case she came back on her own accord. She wasn't there and I started to check the bars outside the neighborhood. I was hoping she hadn't gone downtown, and I knew she didn't have enough carfare to go.

It was ten-thirty before I found her. She was in a little bar on Peacock Street. It was so dark inside I had to stand still for a full minute before my eyes became accustomed to the darkness. There was one customer at the bar and he and the bartender were watching a TV wrestling match. There were two shallow booths opposite the bar and Helen was in the second. A sailor was with her and she was wearing his white sailor hat on the back of her head. His left arm was about her waist, his hand cupping a breast, and his right hand was up under her dress, working furiously. Her legs were spread widely and he was kissing her on the mouth.

I ran directly to the booth, grabbed the sailor by his curly yellow hair and jerked his head back, pulling his mouth away from Helen's. Still keeping a tight grip on his hair I dragged him across her lap to the center of the floor. His body was too heavy to be supported by his hair alone and he slipped heavily to the floor, leaving me with a thick wad of curls in each hand. He mumbled something unintelligible and attempted to sit up. His slack mouth was open and there was a drunken, stupified expression in his eyes. I wanted to hurt him; not kill him, hurt him, mutilate his pasty, slack-jawed face. Looking for a handy weapon, I took a beer bottle from the bar and smashed it over his head. The neck of the bottle was still in my hand and the broken section ended in a long, jagged splinter. I carved his face with it, moving the sharp, glass dagger back and forth across his white face with a whipping wrist motion. Each slash opened a spurting channel of bright red blood that ran down his face and neck and splashed on the floor between his knees. My first blow with the bottle had partially stunned him but the pain brought him out of it and the high screams coming from deep inside his throat were what brought me to my senses. I dropped the piece of broken bottle, and in a way, I felt that I had made up somehow for the degradation I had suffered at the hands of the Marines.

Helen had sobered considerably and her eyes were round as saucers as she sat in the booth. I lifted her to her feet and she started for the door, making a wide detour around the screaming sailor. I opened the door for her and looked over my shoulder. The bartender was nowhere in sight, probably flat on the floor behind the bar. The solitary drinker was peering at me nervously from the safety of the doorway to the men's room. The sailor had managed to get to his knees and was crawling under the table to the first booth, the screams still pouring from his throat. I let the door swing shut behind us.

Helen was able to stand by herself, but both of her hands were pressed over her mouth. I released her arm and she staggered to the curb and vomited into the gutter. When she finished I put my arm around her waist and we walked up the hill. A taxi, coming down the hill on the opposite side of the street, made a U-turn when I signaled him and rolled to a stop beside us. I helped Helen into the cab. A block away from our roominghouse I told the driver to stop. When I opened the door to get out I noticed my hand was cut. I wrapped my handkerchief around my bleeding hand and gave a dollar to the hackie. The cold night air had revived Helen considerably, and she scarcely staggered as we walked the block to the house. As soon as we entered our room she made for the bed and curled up on her knees, pressed her arms to her sides, and ducked her head down. In this position it was difficult for me to remove her clothes, but before I finished taking them off she was asleep.

By that time I could have used a drink myself. I heated the leftover coffee and smoked a cigarette to control my uneasy stomach. I looked through Helen's purse and all I found was a crumpled package of cigarettes and a book of paper matches. Not a penny.

What was the use? I couldn't keep her. How could I work and stay home and watch her at the same time? I couldn't make enough money to meet expenses and keep Helen in liquor if I parked a million cars or fried a million eggs or waited on a million tables. I was so beaten down and disgusted with myself my mind wouldn't cope with it any longer. Sitting awake in the chair I had a dream, a strange, merging dream, where everything was unreal and the ordinary turned into the extraordinary. Nothing like it had ever happened to me before. The coffeepot, the cup, and the can of condensed milk on the table turned into a graphic composition, a depth study. It was beautiful. Everything I turned my eyes upon in the room was perfectly grouped. A professional photographer couldn't have arranged the room any better. The unshaded light in the ceiling was like a light above Van Gogh's pool table. Helen's clothing massed upon the chair swirled gracefully to the floor like drapes in a Titian drawing. The faded gray wallpaper with its unknown red flower pattern was suddenly quaint and charming. The gray background fell away from the flowers with a three-dimensional effect. Everything was lovely, lovely . . .

I don't know how long this spell lasted, but it seemed to be a long time and I didn't want it to end. I had no thought at all during this period. I merely sensed the new delights of my quiet, ordinary room. Only Helen's gentle, open-mouthed snoring furnished the hum of life to my introspection. And then like a blinding flash of headlights striking my eyes, everything was clear to me. Simple. Plain. Clear.

I didn't have to fight any more.

For instance, a man is crossing the street and an auto mobile almost runs him down. He shakes his fist and curses and says to himself: "That Buick almost hit me!" But it wasn't the Buick that almost hit him; the Buick was merely a vehicle. It was the man or woman driving the Buick who almost hit him. Not the Buick. And that was me. I was the automobile, a machine, a well-oiled vehicle now matured to my early thirties. A machine without a driver. The driver was gone. The machine could now relax and run wherever it might, even into a smash. So what? It could function by itself, by habit, reflex, or whatever it was that made it run. Not only didn't I know, I didn't care any more. It might be interesting for that part of me that used to think things out, to sit somewhere and watch Harry Jordan, the machine, go through the motions. The getting up in the morning, the shaving, the shower, walking, talking, drinking. I. Me. Whatever I was, didn't give a damn any more. Let the body function and the senses sense. The body felt elation. The eyes enjoyed the sudden beauty of the horrible little back bedroom. My mind felt nothing. Nothing at all.

Helen sat up suddenly in bed. She retched. A green streak of fluid burst from her lips and spread over her white breasts. I got a towel from the dresser and wiped her face and chest.

"Use this," and I handed her the towel, "if it hits you again."

"I think I'm all right now," she gasped. I brought her a glass of water and held it to her lips. She shook her head to move her lips away from the glass.

"Oh, Harry, I'm so sick, so sick, so sick, so sick . . ."

"You'll be all right." I set the glass on the table.

"Are you mad at me, Harry?"

"What for?" I was surprised at the question.

"For going out and getting drunk the way I did."

"You were fairly drunk when I left."

"I know, but I shouldn't have gone out like that. That sailor . . . the sailor who was with me didn't mean a thing—"

"Forget it. Go back to sleep."

"Harry, you're the only one I've ever loved. I've never loved anyone but you. And if you got sore at me I don't know what I'd do."

"I'm not angry. Go to sleep."

"You get in bed too."

"Not right now. I'm busy."

"Please, Harry. Please?"

"I'm thinking. You know I'm not going to live very long, Helen. No driver. There isn't any driver, Helen, and the controls are set. And I don't know how long they're going to last."

"What are you talking about?"

"Just that I'm not going to live very long. I quit."

Helen threw the covers back, got out of bed and rushed over to me. I was standing flat-footed by the table. My feet could feel the world pushing up at me from below. Black old cinder. I laughed. Cooling on the outside, fire on the inside and nothing in between. It was easy to feel the world turn beneath my feet. Helen was on her knees, her arms were clasped about my legs. She was talking feverishly, and I put my hand on her head.

"What's the matter, Harry!" She cried. "Are you going to try to kill yourself again? Are you angry with me? Please talk to me! Don't look away like that . . ."

"Yes, Helen," I said calmly. "I'm going to kill myself."

Helen pulled herself up, climbing my body, using my clothes as handholds, pressing her naked body against mine. "Oh, darling, darling," she whimpered. "Let me go first! Don't go away and leave me all alone!"

"All right," I said. I picked her up and carried her to the bed. "I won't leave you behind. I wouldn't do that." I kissed her, stroked her hair. "Go on to sleep, now." Helen closed her eyes and in a moment she was asleep. The tear-streaked lines on her face were drying. I undressed and got into bed beside her. Now I could sleep. The machine would sleep, it would wake, it would do things, and then it would crash, out of control and destroy itself. But first it must run over the little body that slept by its side. The small, pitiful creature with the big sienna eyes and the silver streak in its hair.

As I fell asleep I heard music. I didn't have a radio, but it wasn't the type of music played over the radio anyway. It was wild, cacophonous, and there was an off-beat of drums pounding. My laugh was harsh, rasping. I continued to laugh and the salty taste in my mouth came from the unchecked tears running down my cheeks.

dream world

In my dream I was running rapidly down an enormous piano keyboard. The white keys made music beneath my hurried feet as I stepped on them, but the black keys were stuck together with glue and didn't play. Trying to escape the discordant music of the white keys I tried to run on the black keys, slipping and sliding to keep my balance. Although I couldn't see the end of the keyboard I felt that I must reach the end and that it was possible if I could only run fast enough and hard enough. My foot slipped on a rounded black key and I fell heavily, sideways, and my sprawled body covered three of the large white keys with a sharp, harsh discord. The notes were loud and ugly. I rolled away from the piano keyboard, unable to stand, and fell into a great mass of silent, swirling, billowing yellow fog and floated down, down, down. The light surrounding my head was like bright, luminous gold. The gloves on my hand were lemon yellow chamois with three black stitches on the back of each hand. I disliked the gloves, but I couldn't take them off no matter how hard I tried. They were glued to my hands; the bright orange glue oozed out of the glove around my wrists.

I opened my eyes and I was wide awake. My body was drenched with perspiration. I got out of bed without waking Helen, found and lighted a cigarette. My mouth was so dry the smoke choked me and tasted terrible. The perspiration drying on my body made me shiver with cold and I put my shirt and trousers on.

What a weird, mixed-up dream to have! I recalled each sequence of the dream vividly and it didn't make any sense at all. Helen, still asleep, turned and squirmed under the covers. She missed the warmth of my body and was trying to get close to me in her sleep. I crushed my foul-tasting cigarette in the ash-tray and tucked the covers in around Helen. I turned on the overhead light and sat down.

I felt calm and contented. It was time for Harry Jordan to have another cigarette. As though I sat in a dark theatre as a spectator somewhere I observed the quiet, studied actions of Harry Jordan. The exacting, unconscious ritual of putting the cigarette in his mouth, the striking of the match on his thumbnail, the slow withdrawal of smoke, the sensuous exhalation and the obvious enjoyment. The man, Harry Jordan, was a very collected individual, a man of the world. Nothing bothered him now. He was about to withdraw his presence from the world and depart on a journey into space, into nothingness. Somewhere, a womb was waiting for him, a dark, warm place where the living was easy, where it was effortless to get by. A wonderful place where a man didn't have to work or think or talk or listen or dream or cavort or play or use artificial stimulation. A kind old gentleman with a long dark cloak was waiting for him. Death. Never had Death appeared so attractive. . . .

I looked at Helen's beautiful face. She slept peacefully, her mouth slightly parted, her pretty hair tousled. I would take Helen with me. This unfeeling world was too much for Helen too, and without me, who would care for her, look after her? And hadn't I promised to take her with me?

I crushed my cigarette decisively and crossed to the bed.

"Helen, baby," I said, shaking her gently by the shoulder. "Wake up."

She stirred under my hand, snapped her eyes open, awake instantly, the perfect animal. She wore a sweet, sleepy smile.

"What time is it?"

"I don't know," I said, "but it's time." My face was as stiff as cardboard and it felt as expressionless as uncarved stone. I didn't know and didn't want to explain what I was going to do and I hoped Helen wouldn't ask me any questions. She didn't question me. Somehow, she knew instinctively. Perhaps she read the thoughts in my eyes, maybe she could see my intentions in the stiffness of my smile.

"We're going away, aren't we, Harry?" Helen's voice was small, childlike, yet completely unafraid.

Not daring to trust my voice, I nodded. Helen's trust affected me deeply. In that instant I loved her more than I had ever loved her before. Such faith and trust were almost enough to take the curse out of the world. Almost.

"All right, Harry. I'm ready." She closed her eyes and the sleepy winsome smile remained on her lips.

I put my hands around her slender neck. My long fingers interlaced behind her neck and my thumbs dug deeply into her throat, probing for a place to stop her breathing. I gradually increased the pressure, choking her with unrelenting firmness of purpose, concentrating. She didn't have an opportunity to make a sound. At first she thrashed about and then her body went limp. Her dark sienna eyes, flecked with tiny spots of gold, stared guilelessly at me and then they didn't see me any more. I closed her eyelids with my thumb, pulled the covers down and put my ear to her chest. No sound came from her heart. I straightened her legs and folded her arms across her chest. They wouldn't stay folded and I had to place a pillow on top of them before they would stay. Later on, I supposed, when her body stiffened with cold, her arms would stay in place without the benefit of the pillow.

My legs were weak at the knees and I had to sit down to stop their trembling. My fingers were cramped and I opened and closed my hands several times to release the tension. I had taken the irrevocable step and had met Death half-way. I could feel his presence in the room. It was now my turn and, with the last tugs of primitive self-preservation, I hesitated, my conscious mind casting about for a way to renege. But I knew that I wouldn't renege; it was unthinkable. It was too late to back out now. However, I didn't have the courage and trust that Helen had possessed. There was no one kind enough to take charge of the operation or do it for me. I had to do it myself, without help from anyone. But I had to have a little something to help me along . . .

I omitted the socks and slipped into my shoes. I couldn't control my hands well enough to tie the laces and I let them hang loose. I put my jacket on and left my room, locked the door, and left for the street. It was dismally cold outside; there were little patches of fog swirling in groups like lost ghosts exploring the night streets. The traffic signals at the corner were turned off for the night; only the intermittent blinking of the yellow caution lights at the four corners of the intersection lighted the lost, drifting tufts of fog. Although it was after one, Mr. Watson's delicatessen was still open. Its brightly colored window was a warm spot on the dark line of buildings. I crossed the street and entered and the tinkling bell above the door announced my entrance. Mrs. Watson was sitting in a comfortable chair by the counter reading a magazine. She was a heavy woman with orange-tinted hair and a faint chestnut moustache. She smiled at me in recognition.

"Hello Harry," she said, "How are you this evening?"

"Fine, Mrs. Watson, just fine," I replied. I was glad that it was Mrs. Watson instead of her husband in the shop that morning. I wanted to talk to somebody and she was much easier to talk to than her husband. He was a German immigrant and it always seemed to me like he considered it a favor when he waited on me. I fished the two one dollar bills out of my watch pocket and smoothed them out flat on the counter.

"I think I'm getting a slight cold, Mrs. Watson," I said, coughing into my curled fist, "and I thought if I made a little hot gin punch before I went to bed it might cut the phlegm a little bit."

"Nothing like hot gin for colds." Mrs. Watson smiled and

got out of the chair to cross to the liquor shelves. "What kind?"

"Gilbey's is fine—I'd like a pint, but I don't think I have enough here . . ." I pointed to the two one dollar bills.

"I think I can trust you for the rest, Harry. It wouldn't be the first time." She dropped a pint of Gilbey's into a sack, twisted the top and handed it to me. I slipped the bottle into my jacket pocket. My errand was over and I could leave, but I was reluctant to leave the warm room and the friendly, familiar delicatessen smells. Death was waiting for me in my room. I had an appointment with him and I meant to keep it, but he could wait a few minutes longer.

"What are you reading, Mrs. Watson?" I asked politely, when she had returned to her chair after ringing a No Sale on the cash register and putting my money into the drawer.

"*Cosmopolitan.*" Her pleasant laugh was tinged with irony. "Boy meets girl, loses girl, gets girl. They're all the same, but they pass the time."

"That's a mighty fine magazine, Mrs. Watson. I read it all the time; and so does my wife. Why, Helen can hardly wait for it to come out and we always argue over who gets to read it first and all that. Yes, I guess it's my favorite magazine and I wish it was published every week instead of every month! What month is that, Mrs. Watson? Maybe I haven't read it yet."

"Do you feel all right, Harry?" She looked at me suspiciously.

"Yes, I do." My voice had changed pitch and was much too high.

"You aren't drunk, are you?"

"No, I get a little talkative sometimes. Well, that's a good magazine."

"It's all right." Mrs. Watson's voice was impatient; she wanted to get back to her story.

"Well good night, Mrs. Watson, and thanks a lot." I opened the door.

"That's all right, Harry. Good night." She had found her place and was reading before I closed the door.

As soon as I was clear of the lighted window I jerked the gin out of the sack, tossed the sack in the gutter, and unscrewed the cap from the bottle. I took a long pull from the bottle, gulping the raw gin down until I choked on it and hot tears leaped to my eyes. It warmed me through and my head cleared immediately. I crossed the street and walked back to the house. Sitting on the outside steps I drank the rest of the gin in little sips, controlling my impulse to down it all at once. I knew that if I tried to let it all go down my throat at once it would be right back up and the effects would be gone. I finished the bottle and tossed it into the hedge by the porch. My stomach had a fire inside it, but I was sorry I hadn't charged a fifth instead of only getting a pint.

I walked down the dimly lighted hall, unlocked my door and entered my room. It rather startled me, in a way, to see Helen in the same position I had left her in. Not that I had expected her to move; I hadn't expected anything, but to see her lying so still, and uncovered in the cold room, unnerved me. Again I wished I had another pint of gin. I started to work.

I locked the door and locked the window. There were three old newspapers under the sink and I tore them into strips and stuffed the paper under the crack at the bottom of the door. I opened both jets on the two-ring burner and they hissed full blast. I sniffed the odor and it wasn't unpleasant at all. It was sweet and purifying. By this time the gin had hit me hard, and I found myself humming a lit-tle tune. I undressed carefully and hung my clothes neatly in the closet. I lined my shoes up at the end of the bed. Tomorrow we would be found dead and that was that. But there wasn't any note. I staggered to the table and with a piece of charcoal I composed a brief note of farewell. There was no one in particular to address it to, so I headed it:

> To Who Finds This:
> We did this on purpose. It isn't accidental.

I couldn't think of anything else to put in the note and I didn't sign it because the charcoal broke between my fin-gers. Leaving the note on the table I crawled into bed beside Helen and pulled the covers up over us both. I had left the overhead light on purposely and the room seemed gay and cheerful. I took Helen in my arms and kissed her.

Her lips were like cold rubber. When I closed my eyes the image of the light bulb remained. I tried to concentrate on other things to induce sleep. The black darkness of the outside street, the inky San Francisco bay, outside space and starless skies. There were other thoughts that tried to force their way into my mind but I fought them off successfully.

The faint hissing of the gas jets grew louder. It filled the room like a faraway waterfall.

I was riding in a barrel and I could hear the falls far away. It was a comfortable barrel, well-padded, and it rocked gently to and fro, comforting me. It floated on a broad stream, drifting along with the current. The roar of the falls was louder in my ears. The barrel was drifting closer to the falls, moving ever faster toward the boiling steam above the lips of the overhang. I wondered how far the drop would be. The barrel hesitated for a second, plunged downward with a sickening drop.

A big black pair of jaws opened and I dropped inside. They snapped shut.

awakening 14

There was a lot of knocking and some shouting. I don't know whether it was the knocking or the shouting that aroused me from my deep, restful slumbers, but I awoke, and printed in large, wavering red letters on the surface of my returning consciousness was the word for Harry Jordan: *FAILURE*. Somehow, I wasn't surprised. Harry Jordan was a failure in everything he tried. Even suicide.

The sharp little raps still pounded on the door and I could hear Mrs. McQuade's anxious voice calling, "Mr. Jordan! Mr. Jordan! Open the door."

"All right!" I shouted from the bed. "Wait a minute."

I painfully got out of bed, crossed to the window, unlocked it and threw it open. The cold, damp air that rushed in from the alley smelled like old laundry. The gas continued to hiss from the two open burners and I turned them off. Again the rapping and the call from Mrs. McQuade: "Open the door!"

"In a minute!" I replied. The persistent knocking and shouting irritated me. I slipped into my corduroy trousers, buckled my belt as I crossed the room, unlocked and opened the door. Mrs. McQuade and her other two star roomers, Yoshi Endo and Miss Foxhall, were framed in the doorway. It's a composition by Paul Klee, I thought.

I had always thought of Mrs. McQuade as a garrulous old lady with her hand held out, but she took charge of the situation like a television director.

"I smelled the gas," Mrs. McQuade said quietly. "Are you all right?"

"I guess so."

"Go stand by the window and breathe some fresh air."

"Maybe I'd better." I walked to the window and took a few deep breaths which made me cough. After the coughing fit I was giddier than before. I turned and looked at Endo and Miss Foxhall. "Won't you please come in?" I asked them stupidly.

Little Endo, his dark eyes bulging like a toad's in his flat Oriental face, stared solemnly at Helen's naked figure on the bed. Miss Foxhall had covered her face with both hands and was peering through the lattice-work of her fingers. Mrs. McQuade examined Helen for a moment at the bedside and then she pulled the covers over the body and face. Pursing her lips, she turned and made a flat, quiet statement: "She's dead."

"Yes," I said. Just to be doing something, anything, I put my shirt on, sat down in the straight chair and pulled on my socks. A shrill scream escaped Miss Foxhall and then she stopped herself by shoving all her fingers into her mouth. Her short involuntary scream brought Endo out of his trance-like state and he grabbed the old spinster's arm and began to shake her, saying over and over again in a high, squeaky voice, "No, no! No, no!"

"Leave her alone," Mrs. McQuade ordered sharply. "I'll take care of her." She put an arm around Mrs Foxhall's waist. "You go get a policeman." Endo turned and ran down the hall. I heard the outside door slam. As Mrs. McQuade led Miss Foxhall away, she said over her shoulder: "You'd better get dressed, Mr. Jordan."

"Yes, M'am." I was alone with Helen and the room was suddenly, unnaturally quiet. Automatically, I finished dressing, but my hands trembled so much I wasn't able to tie my necktie. I let it hang loosely around my neck, and sat down in the straight chair after I donned my jacket.

Why had I failed?

I sat facing the door and I looked up and saw the transom. It was open. It wasn't funny but I smiled grimly. No wonder the gas hadn't killed me. The escaping gas was too busy going out over the transom and creeping through the house calling attention to Harry Jordan in the back bedroom. How did I let it happen? To hold the gas in the room I had shoved newspaper under the bottom of the door and yet I had left the transom wide open. Was it a primeval desire to live? plain stupidity? or the effects of the gin? I'll never know.

In a few minutes Endo returned to the room with a policeman. The policeman was a slim, nervous young man and he stood in the doorway covering me with his revolver. More than a little startled by the weapon I raised my arms over my head. The policeman bit his lips while his sharp eyes roved the room, sizing up the situation. He holstered the pistol and nodded his head.

"Put your arms down," he ordered. "Little suicide pact, huh?"

"No," I replied. "I killed her. Choked her to death." I folded my hand in my lap.

The young policeman uncovered Helen's head and throat and looked carefully at her neck. Endo was at his side and the proximity of the little Japanese bothered him. He pushed Endo roughly toward the door. "Get the hell out of here," he told Endo. Leaving the room reluctantly, Endo hovered in the doorway. Muttering under his breath, the policeman shut the door in Endo's face and seated himself on the foot of the bed.

"What's your name?" He asked me, taking a small, black notebook out of his hip pocket.

"Harry Jordan."

"Her name?" He jerked his thumb over his shoulder.

"Mrs. Helen Meredith."

"You choked her. Right?"

"Yes."

"And then you turned on the gas to kill yourself?"

"Yes."

"She doesn't looked choked."

"There's the note I left," I s   pointing to the table. He crossed to the table and read my charcoaled note without touching it. He made another notation in his little black book, returned it to his hip pocket.

"Okay, okay, okay," he said meaninglessly. There was uncertainty in his eyes. "I've got to get my partner," he informed me. Evidently he didn't know whether to take me along or leave me in the room by myself. He decided on the latter and handcuffed me to the radiator and hurried out of the room, closing the door behind him. The radiator was too low for me to stand and I had to squat down. Squatting nauseated me, and I got down on my knees on the floor. There was a queasy feeling in the pit of my stomach and it rumbled, but I didn't get sick enough to throw up.

In a few minutes he was back with his partner. He was a much older, heavier policeman, with a buff-colored, neatly trimmed mustache and a pair of bright, alert hazel eyes. The older man grinned when he saw me handcuffed to the radiator.

"Take the cuffs off him, for Christ sake!" he told the younger policeman. "He won't get away."

After the first policeman uncuffed me and returned the heavy bracelets to his belt, I sat down in the chair again. By leaning over and sucking in my stomach I could keep the nausea under control. It was much better sitting down. The younger policeman left the room to make a telephone call and the older man took his place at the foot of the bed. He crossed his legs and after he got his cigarettes out he offered me one. He displayed no interest in Helen's body at all. He lit our cigarettes and then smiled kindly at me.

"You're in trouble, boy," he said, letting smoke trickle out through his nose. "Do you know that?"

"I guess I am." I took a long drag and it eased my stomach.

"Relax, boy. I'm not going to ask you any questions. I couldn't care less."

"Would it be all right with you if I kissed her goodbye?" That question slipped out in a rush, but he seemed to be easy-going, and I knew that after the police arrived in force I wouldn't be able to kiss her goodbye. This would be my last chance. He scratched his mustache, got up from the bed and strolled across the room to the window.

"I suppose it's all right" he said thoughtfully. "What do you want to kiss her for?"

"Just kiss her goodbye. That's all." I couldn't explain because I didn't know myself.

"Okay." He shrugged his shoulders and looked out the window. "Go ahead."

Walking bent over I crossed to the bed and kissed Helen's cold lips, her forehead, and on the lips again. "Goodbye, sweetheart," I whispered low enough so the policeman couldn't hear me, "I'll see you soon." I returned to the chair.

For a long time we sat quietly in the silent room. The door opened and the room was filled with people. It was hard to believe so many people could crowd into such a small room. There were the two original uniformed policemen, two more in plainclothes, a couple of hospital attendants or doctors in white—Endo got back into the room somehow—Mrs. McQuade, and a spectator who had crowded in from the group in front of the house. A small man entered the room and removed his hat. He was almost bald and wore a pair of dark glasses. At his entrance the room was quiet again and the noise and activity halted. The young policeman saluted smartly and pointed to me.

"He confessed, Lieutenant," the young man said. "Harry Jordan is his name and she isn't his wife—"

"I'll talk to him," the little man said, holding up a white, manicured hand. He removed the dark glasses and put them in the breast pocket of his jacket, crooked his finger at me and left the room. I followed him out and nobody tried to stop me. We walked down the hall and he paused at the stairway leading to the top floor.

"Want a cigarette, Jordan?"

"No, sir."

"Want to tell me about it, Jordan?" He asked with his quiet voice. "I'm always a little leery of confessions unless I hear them myself."

"Yes, sir. There isn't much to tell. I choked her last night, and then I turned on the gas. It was a suicide pact, in a way, but actually I killed Helen because she didn't have the nerve to do it herself."

"I see. About what time did it happen?"

"Around one, or after. I don't know. By this time I would have been dead myself if I hadn't left the transom open."

"You willing to put all this on paper, Jordan, or are you going to get a shyster and deny everything, or what?"

"I'm guilty, Lieutenant, and I want to die. I'll cooperate in every way I can. I don't want to see a lawyer, I just want to be executed. It'll be easier that way all around."

"Then that's the way it'll be." He raised his hand and a plainclothesman came down the hall, handcuffed me to his wrist, and we left the rooming-house. A sizeable crowd had gathered on the sidewalk and they stared at us curiously as we came down the outside steps and entered the waiting police car. A uniformed policeman drove us to the city jail.

At the desk I was treated impersonally by the booking sergeant. He filled in my name, address, age and height and then asked me to dump my stuff on the desk and remove my belt and shoelaces. There wasn't much to put on the desk. A piece of string, a thin, empty wallet, a parking stub left over from the Continental Garage, a button and a dirty handkerchief were all I had to offer. I put them on the desk and removed my belt and shoelaces, added them to the little pile. The sergeant wrote my name on a large brown manila envelope and started to fill it with my possessions.

"I'd like to keep the wallet, Sergeant," I said. He went through it carefully. All it contained was a small snapshot of Helen taken when she was seven years old. The little snapshot showed a girl in a white dress and Mary Jane slippers standing in the sunlight in front of a concrete bird-bath. Her eyes were squinted against the sun and she stood pigeontoed, with her hands behind her back. Once in a while, I liked to look at it. The sergeant tossed me the wallet with the picture and I shoved it into my pocket.

I was fingerprinted, pictures were taken of my face, profile and full-face, and then I was turned over to the jailer. He was quite old, and walked with an agonized limp. We entered the elevator, were whisked up several floors, and then he led me down a long corridor to the shower room.

After I undressed and folded my clothes neatly on the wooden bench I got under the shower and adjusted the water as hot as I could stand it. The water felt wonderful. I let the needle streams beat into my upturned face. It sluiced down over my body, warming me through and through. I soaped myself roughly with the one-pound cake of dark-brown laundry soap, stood under the hot water again.

I toweled myself with an olive drab towel and dressed in the blue pants and blue work shirt that were laid out on the bench. The trousers were too large around the waist and I had to hold them up with one hand. I followed Mr. Benson the jailer to the special block and he opened the steel door and locked it behind us. We walked down the narrow corridor to the last cell. He unlocked the door, pointed, and I entered. He clanged the door to, locked it with his key. As he turned to leave I hit him up for a smoke. He passed a cigarette through the bars, lighted it for me with his Zippo lighter.

"I suppose you've had breakfast already," he said gruffly.

"No, but I'm not hungry anyway."

"You mean you couldn't stand a cup of coffee?"

"I suppose I could drink a cup of coffee all right."

"I'll get you one then. No use playing coy with me. When you want something you gotta speak up. I ain't no mind-reader."

He limped away and I could hear the slap-and-drag of his feet all the way down the corridor. While I waited for the coffee I investigated my cell. The walls were gray, freshly-painted, but the paint didn't cover all of the obscene drawings and initials beneath the paint where former occupants had scratched their records. I read some of the inscriptions: FRISCO KID '38, H. E., J. D., KILROY WAS HERE, Smoe, DENVER JACK, and others. Along the length of the entire wall, chest high, in two inch letters, someone had cut deeply into the plaster:

UP YOUR RUSTY DUSTY WITH A FLOY FLOY

This was very carefully carved. It must have taken the prisoner a long time to complete it.

A porcelain toilet, without a wooden seat, a washbowl

with one spigot of cold water, and a tier of three steel beds with thin cotton pads for mattresses completed the inventory of the cell. No window. I unfastened the chains and let the bottom bunk down. I sat down on it and finished half my cigarette. Instead of throwing the butt away I put it into my shirt pocket. It was all I had. Presently, Mr. Benson came back with my coffee and passed the gray enameled cup through the bars.

"I didn't know whether you liked it with sugar and cream so I brought it black," he said.

"That's fine." I took the cup gratefully and sipped it. It was almost boiling hot and I had to let it cool some before I could finish it, but Mr. Benson waited patiently. When I passed him the empty cup he gave me a fresh sack of tobacco and a sheaf of brown cigarette papers.

"Know how to roll 'em, Jordan?"

"Sure. Thanks a lot." I made a cigarette.

"You get issued a sack every day, but no matches. If you want a light you gotta holler. Okay?"

"Sure." Mr. Benson lit my cigarette and limped away again down the hollow-sounding corridor. The heavy end door clanged and locked.

The reaction set in quickly, the reaction to Helen's death, my attempt at suicide, the effects of the liquor, all of it. It was the overall cumulation of events that hit me all at once. My knees, my legs, my entire body began to shake violently and I couldn't control any part of it. The wet cigarette fell apart in my hand and I dropped to my knees in a praying position. I started to weep, at first soundlessly, then blubbering, the tears rolled down my cheeks, streamed onto my shirt. Perspiration poured from my body. I prayed:

"Dear God up there! Put me through to Helen! I'm still here, baby! Do you hear me! Please hang on a little while and wait for me! I'll be with you as soon as they send me! I'm all alone now, and it's hard, hard, hard! I'll be with you soon, soon, soon! I love you! Do you you hear me, sweetheart? I love you! I LOVE YOU!"

From one of the cells down the corridor a thick gutteral voice answered mine: "And I love you, too!" The voice paused, added disgustedy: "Why don't you take a goddam break for Christ's sake!"

I stopped praying, or talking to Helen, whatever I was doing, and stretched out full length on the concrete floor. I stretched my arms out in front of me and pressed my mouth against the cold floor. In that prone position I cried myself out, silently, and it took a long time. I didn't try to pull myself together, because I knew that I would never cry again.

Afterwards, I washed my face with the cold tap water at the washbowl and dried my wet face with my shirt tail. I sat down on the edge of my bunk and carefully tailored another cigarette. It was a good one, nice and fat and round. Getting to my feet I crossed to the barred door.

"Hey! Mr. Benson!" I shouted. "How's about a light?"

confession 15

Lunch consisted of beef stew, rice, stewed apricots and coffee. After the delayed-action emotional ordeal I had undergone I was weak physically and I ate every scrap of food on my aluminum tray. With my stomach full, for the first time in weeks, I lay down on the bottom bunk, covered myself with the clean gray blanket and fell asleep immediately.

Mr. Benson aroused me at four-thirty by rattling an empty cup along the bars of my cell. It was time to eat again. The supper was a light one; fried mush, molasses and coffee with a skimpy dessert of three stewed prunes. Again I cleaned the tray, surprised at my hunger. I felt rested, contented, better than I had felt in months. My headache had all but disappeared and the peaceful solitude of my cell was wonderful. Mr. Benson picked up the tray and gave me a book of paper matches before he left. He was tired of walking the length of the corridor to light my cigarettes. I lay on my back on the hard bunk and enjoyed my cigarette. After I stubbed it out on the floor I closed my eyes. When I opened them again it was morning and Mr. Benson was at the bars with my breakfast. Two pieces of bread, a thimble-sized paper cupful of strawberry jam and a cup of coffee.

About an hour after breakfast the old jailer brought a razor and watched me shave with the cold water and the brown laundry soap. In another hour he brought my clothes to the cell. My corduroy slacks and jacket had been sponged and pressed and were fairly presentable.

"Your shirt's in the laundry," he said, "but you can wear your tie with the blue shirt."

"Where am I going?" I asked as I changed clothes.

"The D.A. wants to talk to you. Just leave them blue work pants on the bunk. You gotta change when you get back anyways."

"Okay," I agreed. I tied my necktie as well as I could without a mirror, just as I had shaved without a mirror. I followed Mr. Benson's limping drag down the corridor and this time I took an interest in the other prisoners in the special block, looking into each cell as I passed. There were eight cells, all of them along one side facing the passage wall, but only two others in addition to mine were occupied with prisoners. One held a sober-looking middle-aged man sitting on his bunk staring at his steepled fingers, and the other held a spiky-haired, blond youth with a broken nose and one cocked violet eye. He cocked it at me as I passed the cell and his sullen face was without expression. I quickly concluded that he was the one who had mocked me the day before and I had an overwhelming desire to kick his teeth in.

A plainclothes detective, wearing his hat, met us at the end of the corridor, signed for me, cuffed me to his wrist and we walked down the hall to the elevator. We silently rode the elevator down to the third floor, got out, and walked down a carpeted hallway to a milk-glass door with a block-lettered inscription. Asst District Atty San Francisco. We entered the office and the detective removed the cuff and left the room. The office was small and shabbily furnished. There was a battered, oak desk, a shelf of heavy law books, four straight chairs and a row of hunting prints on the sepia-tinted wall across from the bookshelf. The prints were all of gentlewomen, sitting their horses impossibly and following hounds over a field-stone wall. All four prints were exactly the same. I sat down in one of the chairs and a moment later two men entered. The first through the door was a young man with very white skin and a blue-black beard hovering close to the surface of his chin. It was the kind of beard that shows, because I could tell by the scraped skin on his jaws that he had shaved that morning. He wore a shiny, blue gabardine suit and oversized glasses with imitation tortoise-shell rims. Business-like, he sat behind the desk and studied some papers in a folder. The other man was quite old. He had lank white hair drooping down over his ears and there was a definite tremor in his long, talon-like fingers. His suit coat and trousers didn't match and he carried a shorthand pad and several sharp-ened pencils. It seemed unusual to me that the city would employ such an old man as a stenographer. His white head nodded rapidly up and down and it never stopped its meaningless bobbing throughout the interview, but his deepset eyes were bright and alert and without glasses.

The younger man closed the folder and shoved it into the top drawer of his desk. His eyes fastened on mine and without taking them away he extracted a king-sized ciga-rette from the package on the desk, flipped the desk lighter and the flame found the end of the cigarette perfectly. He did this little business without looking away from my eyes at all. A movie gangster couldn't have done it better. After three contemplative drags on the cigarette he crushed it out in the glass ash-tray, rested his elbows on the desk, cradled his square chin in his hands and leaned forward.

"My name is Robert Seely." His voice was deep and reso-nant with a lot of college speech training behind it. "I'm one of the assistant District Attorneys and your case has been assigned to me." He hesitated, and for a moment I thought he was going to shake hands with me, but he didn't make such an offer. He changed his steady gaze to the old man.

"Are you ready, Timmy?"

The old man, Timmy, held up his pencils and notebook in reply.

"I want to ask you a few questions," Robert Seely said. "Your name is . . . ?"

"Harry Jordan."

"And your residence?"

I gave him my roominghouse address.

"Occupation?"

"Art teacher."

"Place of employment?"

"Unemployed."

"What was the name of the woman you murdered?"

"Helen Meredith. Mrs. Helen Meredith."

"What was she doing in your room?"

"She lived there . . . the past few weeks."

"Where is her husband, Mr. Meredith?"

"I don't know. She said something once about him living in San Diego, but she wasn't sure of it."

"Did Mrs. Meredith have another address here in the city?"

"No. Before she moved to San Francisco she lived with her mother in San Sienna. I don't know that address either, but her mother's name is Mrs. Mathews. I don't know the first name."

"All right. Take one." He pushed the package of cigarettes across the desk and I removed one and lighted it with the desk lighter. Mr. Seely held the open package out to the ancient stenographer.

"How can I smoke and take this down too?" The old man squeaked peevishly.

"Why did you kill Mrs. Meredith?" Mr. Seely asked me.

"Well, I . . ." I hesitated.

"Before we go any further, Jordan, I think I'd better tell you that anything you say may be held against you. Do you understand that?"

"You should've told him that before," the old man said sarcastically.

"I'm handling this interview, Timmy," Mr. Seely said coldly. "Your job is to take it down. Now, Jordan, are you aware that what you say may be held against you?"

"Of course. I don't care about that."

"Why then, did you kill Mrs. Meredith?"

"In a way, it's a long story."

"Just tell it in your own words."

"Well, we'd been drinking, and once before we'd tried suicide and it didn't work so we went to the hospital and asked for psychiatric help."

"What hospital was that?"

"Saint Paul's. We stayed for a week, that is, Helen was in a week. I was only kept for three days."

"How did you attempt suicide?"

"With a razor blade." I held my arms over the desk, showing him the thin red scars on my wrists. "The psychiatric help we received was negligible. We started to drink as soon as we were released from the hospital. Anyway, I couldn't work very well and drink too. The small amount of money I made wouldn't stretch and I was despondent all the time."

"And was Mrs. Meredith despondent, too?"

"She always took my moods as her own. If I was happy, she was happy. We were perfectly compatible in every respect—counterparts, rather. So that's how I happened to kill her, you see. She knew all along I was going to kill myself sooner or later and she made me promise to kill her first. So I did. Afterwards I turned on the gas. The next thing I knew, Mrs. McQuade—that's my landlady—was hollering and pounding on the door. My—Helen was dead and I wasn't." With food in my stomach and a good night's sleep and a cigarette in my hand it was easy for me to talk about it.

"I have your suicide note, Jordan, and I notice it's written in charcoal. In the back of your mind, did you have an idea you could rub the charcoal away in case the suicide didn't work? Why did you use charcoal?"

"I didn't have a pencil."

Timmy chuckled at my reply, avoided Mr. Seely's icy stare and bent over his notebook.

"Then the death of Mrs. Meredith was definitely premeditated?"

"Yes, definitely. I plead guilty to everything, anything."

"Approximately what time was it when you choked her?"

"I don't know exactly. Somewhere between one and two a.m. Right afterwards I went out and got a pint of gin at the delicatessen down the street. It must have been before two or it wouldn't have been open."

"What delicatessen?"

"Mr. Watson's. Mrs. Watson sold me the gin, though. I still owe her forty-three cents."

"All right. We'll check the time with her. The police arrested you at ten minutes after eight. If you actually intended to commit suicide, why did you leave your transom open?"

"I don't know. I must have forgot about it, I guess."

"Did you drink the pint of gin?"

"It was a cold night, and I needed something to warm me up."

"I see. Where did you teach art last? You said you were an—"

"Lately I've been working around town as a counterman or fry cook."

"Do you have a particular lawyer in mind? I can get in touch with one for you."

"No. I don't need a lawyer. I'm guilty and that's the way I plead. I don't like to go through all this red tape. I expected to be dead by now and all these questions are inconvenient. The sooner I get it over with in the gas chamber the happier I'll be."

"Are you willing to sign a confession to that effect?"

"Certainly. I'll sign anything that'll speed things up."

"How did you and Mrs. Meredith get together in the first place?"

I thought the question over and decided it was none of his business.

Timmy's head stopped bobbing up and down and wagged back and forth from side to side for a change. "He doesn't have to answer questions like that, Mr. Seely," he said in his weak, whining voice. The two men stared at each other distastefully and Timmy won the battle of the eyes.

"Have you got enough for a confession, Timmy?" Mr. Seely asked the old man, at last.

"Plenty." Timmy nodded his white head up and down.

"That's all I have then, Jordan," Mr. Seely said. "No. One more question. Do you want to complain you were mentally unstable at the time? Or do you think you're mentally ill now?"

"Of course not. I'm perfectly sane and I knew what I was

doing at the time. I'd planned it for several weeks."

"You'd better put that in the confession, Timmy." Mr. Seely left the desk and opened the door. The detective was waiting in the hall. "You can return Jordan to his cell now," Mr. Seely told the detective.

I was handcuffed and taken back to the special block and turned over to Mr. Benson. Back into my cell I changed back to my jail clothes and Mr. Benson took my own clothes away on a wire coat hanger. I was alone in my quiet cell.

My mind was much more at ease than it had been before. Thinking back over the interview I felt quite satisfied that the initial step was taken and the ball rolling. Blind justice would filter in and get me sooner or later. It was pleasant to look forward to the gas chamber. What a nice, easy way to die! So painless. Silent and practically odorless and clean! I would sit in a chair, wearing a pair of new black trunks, and stare back at a few rows of spectators staring at me. I would hear nothing and smell nothing. Then I would be dead. When I writhed on the floor and went into convulsions I wouldn't even know about it. Actually, it would be a much more horrible experience for the witnesses than it would be for me. This knowledge gave me a feeling of morbid satisfaction. I had to laugh.

Soon it was time for lunch. Mr. Benson brought a tray to my cell containing boiled cabbage, white meat, bread and margarine, raspberry jello and black coffee. I attacked the food with relish. Food had never tasted better. My mind was relieved now that things were underway and I wasn't eating in a greasy cafe and I hadn't had to cook the food myself. I suppose that is why it all tasted so good. After wiping up the cabbage pot-licker with the last of my bread I rolled and smoked a cigarette. Mr. Benson took the tray away and was back in a few minutes with Old Timmy.

"I've got your confession ready, boy," the old man said.

Timmy signed for me and we left the block for the elevator. After Timmy pushed the button for the third floor, he turned and smiled at me, bobbing his head up and down.

"You aren't sensitive, are you, Jordan?"

"How do you mean," I asked, puzzled.

"Well, it isn't really necessary for me to take you downstairs to sign your confession, and when you aren't in the block you're supposed to wear regular clothes instead of these . . ." He plucked at my blue jail shirt. "And I'm supposed to have a police officer along too." He laughed thinly. "But some of the girls in the office wanted to get a look at you. Funny, the way these young girls go for the *crime passionell*. I didn't think you'd mind."

We walked down the carpeted hallway of the third floor and entered a large office that held five desks, each with telephone and typewriter. Old Timmy winked at me as I nervously looked at the nine women who had crowded into the office. They were all ages, but were still considered girls by Old Timmy.

"This is the steno pool," Timmy said as we crossed to his desk.

"I see it is," I replied.

"I been in charge of this office for thirty-one years." He had seven neatly typed copies of my confession on his desk and I signed them all with a ball point pen. He called two of the girls over to sign on the witness lines and they came forward timidly and signed where he held his talon-like finger. I had the feeling if I said boo the girls would jump through the window. After they signed their names they rejoined the other women, and the silent group stared at me boldly as we left the office. As Timmy shut the door behind us I heard the foolish giggling begin and so did the old man.

"I hope it didn't bother you, boy," he said, "They're just women."

"Yes, I know," I replied meaninglessly.

We entered the elevator again and Timmy pushed the button and looked at me friendlily.

"What do you think of our brilliant Assistant District Attorney, the eminent Mr. Seely?" There were sharp overtones of sarcasm in his thin, whining voice.

"I don't think anything of him," I said. "That is, one way or the other," I amended.

"He's an ass!" Timmy said convincingly. "I'd like to assign him a case."

"It doesn't make any difference to me," I said.

"You should have read your confession, boy. It's iron-tight, you can bet on that. It's a good habit to get into, reading what you sign."

"I'm not making any more habits, good or bad," I said.

Timmy chuckled deep in his throat. "You're right about that!"

We reached the special block and I returned to the custody of Mr. Benson. He opened the heavy end door and Old Timmy shook hands with me before he left, bobbed his head up and down.

He turned away head bobbing, hands jerking, and tottered down the corridor, his feet silent on the concrete floor.

I settled down in my cell to wait. I would be tried as a matter of course, convicted, and go to wait some more in the death row at San Quentin. There, after a prescribed period and on a specified date, I would be executed. And that was that.

I wondered how long it all would take.

sanity test 16

I don't know how long I waited in my quiet cell before I was taken out of it again. It might have been three days, four days or five days. There was no outside light, just the refulgent electric bulbs in my cell and in the corridor. If it hadn't been for the meals, I wouldn't have known the time of day. I didn't worry about the time; I let it slip by unnoticed. I was fed and I was allowed to take a shower every day. And the forty slim cigarettes that can be rolled from a sack of Bull Durham were just enough to last me one full day. Mr. Benson let me have matches when I ran out, and I got by very well. After breakfast one morning, Mr. Benson brought my clothes down to my cell.

"Get dressed, Jordan," he told me, "you're going on a little trip."

"Where to?"

"Get dressed, I said."

My white shirt, stiffly starched, was back from the laundry. I tore off the cellophane wrapping, put it on, my slacks, tied my necktie. The jailer gave me my belt and

shoelaces and I put the laces in my shoes, the belt through
the trouser loops, slipped into my sports jacket.

"Don't you know where I'm going?" I asked.

"Of course I know. Hospital. Observation."

I hesitated at the door of my cell. "Hell, I'm all right. I
don't want to go to any hospital for observation. I signed a
confession; what more do they want?"

"Don't worry about it," Mr. Benson reassured me. "It's
routine. They always send murder suspects to the hospital
nowadays. It's one of the rules."

"It isn't just me then?"

"No. It's routine. Come on, I ain't got all day."

I followed him down the corridor, but my mind didn't
accept his glib explanation. I didn't believe my stay in the
hospital would be very long, but I didn't want them to get
any ideas that I was insane. That would certainly delay my
case and I wanted to get it over with as soon as possible.
Right then, I made up my mind to cooperate with the psychiatrist, no matter what it cost me in embarrassment. It
wouldn't do at all to be found criminally insane and to
spend the rest of my life in an institution.

The detective was the same one who had taken me downstairs for my interview with Mr. Seely. He still had his hat
on, and after he signed for me, and we were riding down in
the elevator, I took a closer look at him. He was big and
tough looking, with the inscrutable look that old time crimi-
nals and old time policemen have in common. To be
friendly, I tried to start a little conversation with the man.

"Those other two guys, the ones in the special block with
me; what are they in for?" I asked him.

"What do you want to know for?"

"Just curious, I suppose."

"You prisoners are all alike. You get in trouble and you
want to hear about others in the same fix. If it makes you
feel any better, I'll tell you this: they're in a lot worse shape
than you are."

We got out of the elevator into the basement and climbed
into the back of a white ambulance that was waiting at the
loading ramp. The window in back was covered with
drawn gray curtains and I couldn't see anything on the way
to the hospital. But on the way, the detective told me about

the other two prisoners, and like he said, they were in worse shape than I was in. The blond young man had killed his mother with an ax in an argument over the car keys, and the middle-aged man had killed his wife and three children with a shotgun and then had lost his nerve and failed to kill himself. It made me ill to hear about the two men and I was sorry I had asked about them.

A white-jacketed orderly met us at the hospital's receiving entrance and signed the slip the detective gave him. He was a husky, young man in his early thirties and there was a broad smile on his face. His reddish hair was closely cropped in a fresh crew-cut and there was a humorous expression in his blue eyes. The detective uncuffed me, put the slip of paper in his pocket and winked at the orderly.

"He's your baby, Hank," he said.

"We'll take good care of him, don't worry," the orderly said good-naturedly and I followed him inside the hospital. We entered the elevator and rode it up to the sixth floor. Hank had to unlock the elevator door with a key before we could leave the elevator. As soon as we were in the hallway he locked the elevator door again and we left the hallway for a long narrow corridor with locked cells on both sides of it. He unlocked the door marked Number 3, and motioned for me to enter. It was a small windowless room and the walls were of unpainted wood instead of gray plaster. There were no bunks, just a mattress on the floor without sheets, and a white, neatly, folded blanket at the foot. The door was made of thick, heavy wood, several layers thick with a small spy-hole at eye-level, about the size of a silver dollar. Hank started to close the door on me and I was terrified, irrationally so.

"Don't!" I said quickly. "Don't shut me up, please! Leave it open, I won't try to run away."

He nodded, smiling. "All right, I'll leave it open a crack. I'm going to get you some pajamas and I'll be back in a few minutes. You start undressing." He closed the door partially and walked away.

I removed my jacket, shirt and pants, and standing naked except for my shoes I waited apprehensively for Hank's return. It wasn't exactly a padded cell, but it was the next thing to it. I was really frightened. For the first time I knew

actual terror. There is a great difference between being
locked in a jail cell and being locked in a madman's cell. At
the jail I was still an ordinary human being, a murderer,
yes, but a normal man locked up in jail with other normal
men. Here, in addition to being a murderer, I was under
serious suspicion, like a dangerous lunatic, under observation from a tiny spy-hole, not to be trusted. Mr. Benson
must have lied to me. Evidently, they thought I was crazy.
Why would they lock me away in such a room if they didn't
think so? I wanted a cigarette to calm my fears, but I didn't
dare call out for one or rap on the door. I was even afraid to
look out the open door, afraid they would think I was trying
to escape, and then I would be put into a padded cell for
sure. From now on I would have to watch out for everything I did, everything I said. Full cooperation. That is what
they would get from me. From now on.

The orderly returned with a pair of blue broadcloth pajamas, a thin white cotton robe and a pair of skivvy slippers.

"Shoes too, Harry," he said.

I sat down on the mattress, removed my shoes and socks
and slid my feet into the skivvy slippers. He dropped my
clothes into a blue sack and pulled the cords tight at the
top. He had a kind face and he winked at me.

"Just take it easy, Harry," he said, "I'll be back in a
minute."

It was a little better having something to cover my naked-
ness. Still, there is a psychological effect to hospital pajamas. Wearing them, a man is automatically a patient, and a
patient is a sick man or he wouldn't be in a hospital. That
was the way I saw it, the only way I could see it. Hank
returned with a syringe and needle and took a blood sample from my right arm. When he turned to leave I asked
him timidly for a cigarette.

"Why, shore," he said and reached into his jacket pocket.
He handed me a fresh package of king-sized Chesterfields
and I opened it quickly, stuck a cigarette in my mouth. He
flipped his lighter for me and said: "Keep the pack." I was
pleased to note that my hands had stopped shaking. "I
can't give you any matches," Hank continued, "but any-
time you want a light or want to go to the can, just holler.
My name is Hank, and I'm at the end of the hall."

"Thanks, Hank," I said appreciatively. "It's nice to smoke tailor-mades again. I've been rolling them at the jail."

"They don't cost me nothing. And when you run out let me know. I can get all I want from the Red Cross." He started to leave with the blood sample, turned and smiled. "Don't worry about the door. I know it's a little rough at first, but I'm right down the hall and if you holler I can hear you. I'll shut the door but I won't latch it. Knowing you aren't locked in is sometimes as good as an open door."

"Will you do that for me?" I asked eagerly.

"Why shore. This maximum security business is a lotta crap anyway. The elevator's locked, there's no stairs, and the windows are all barred, and the door to the roof's locked. No reason to lock your cell." He closed the door behind him, and he didn't lock it.

I sat down on the mattress, my back to the pine wall and chain-smoked three cigarettes. It gave me something to do. If the rest of the staff was as nice to me as Hank I would be able to survive the ordeal and I knew it would be an ordeal. My short stay at Saint Paul's had given me a sample, but now I would be put through the real thing. At noon, Frank brought me my lunch on a tray. There was no knife or fork and I had to eat the lunch with a spoon. The food was better than the jail food, pork chops, french fries and ice cream, but it almost gagged me to eat it. I forced myself to clean the tray and saved the milk for the last. I gulped the milk down with one long swallow, hoping it would clear away the food that felt caught in my throat. When Hank returned for the tray he gave me a light for my smoke. He was pleased when he saw the empty tray.

"That's the way, Harry," he nodded and smiled good-naturedly. "Eat all you can. A man feels better with a full gut. The doctor'll be back after a while and he'll talk to you then. Don't let him worry you. He's a weirdie. All these psychiatrists are a little nuts themselves."

"I'll try not to let it bother me," I said. "How long are they going to keep me here, anyway?"

"I don't know." He grinned. "That all depends."

"You mean it all depends on me?"

"That's right. And the doctor." He left with the tray, closing the door.

About one-thirty or two Hank returned for me and we left the cell and corridor and entered a small office off the main hallway. The office wasn't much larger than my cell, but it contained a barred window that let in a little sunlight. Through the window I could observe the blue sky and the bright green plot of grass in the park outside the hospital. The doctor was seated behind his desk and he pointed to the chair across from it.

"Sit down, Jordan," he said. "Hank, you can wait outside."

There was a trace of accent in his voice. German, maybe Austrian. It was cultivated, but definitely foreign. That is the way it is in the United States. A native born American can't make a decent living and here was a foreigner all set to tell me what was wrong with me. He had a swarthy sun-lamp tan and his black beard was so dark it looked dyed. It was an Imperial beard and it made him resemble the early photographs of Lenin.

"Your beard makes you look like Lenin," I said.

"Why thank you, thank you!" He took it as a compliment. I distrusted the man. There is something about a man with a beard I cannot stand. No particular reason for it. Prejudice, I suppose. I feel the same way about cats.

"I'm Doctor Fischbach," the doctor said unsmilingly. "You're to be here under my observation for a few days." He studied a sheaf of papers, clipped together with large-sized paper clips, for a full five minutes while I sat there under pressure feeling the perspiration rolling freely down my back and under my arms to the elbows. He wagged his bearded chin from side to side, clucked sympathetically.

"Too bad you entered Saint Paul's for help, Jordan." He continued to shake his head. "If you and Mrs. Meredith had come to me in the first place you would have been all right."

"Yeah," I said noncommittally. "You may be right."

"Did Saint Paul's give you any tests of any kind? If so, we could obtain them and save the time of taking them over."

"No, I didn't get any tests—just blood tests."

"Then let us begin with the Rorschach." Dr. Fischbach opened his untidy top desk drawer, dug around in its depths and brought out a stack of cards about six inches by six inches and set them before me, Number One on top. "These are ink blots, Jordan, as you can see. We'll go through the cards one by one and you tell me what they remind you of. Now, how about this one?" He shoved the first card across the desk and I studied it for a moment or so. It looked like nothing.

"It looks like an art student's groping for an idea." I suggested.

"Yes?" He encouraged me.

"It isn't much of anything. Sometimes, Doctor, when an artist is stuck for an idea, he'll doodle around with charcoal to see if he can come up with something. The meaningless lines and mass forms sometimes suggest an idea, and he can develop it into a picture. That's what these ink blots look like to me."

"How about right here?" He pointed with his pencil to one of the larger blots. "Does this look like a butterfly to you?"

"Not to me. No."

"What does it look like?"

"It looks like some artist has been doodling around with black ink trying to get an idea." How many times did he want me to tell him?

"You don't see a butterfly?" He seemed to be disappointed.

"No butterfly." I wanted to cooperate, but I couldn't see any point in lying to the man. It was some kind of trick he was trying to pull on me. I stared hard at the card again, trying to see something, some shape, but I couldn't. None of the blots made a recognizable shape. I shook my head as he went on to the next card which also had four strangely shaped blots.

"Do these suggest anything?" He asked hopefully.

"Yeah," I said. If he wanted to trick me I would play one on him. "I see a chicken in a sack with a man on its back; a bottle of rum and I'll have some; a red-winged leek, and an oversized beak; a pail of water and a farmer's daughter; a bottle of gin and a pound of tin; a false-faced friend and days without end; a big brown bear and he's going everywhere; a big banjo and a—"

He jerked the cards from the desk and shoved them into the drawer. He looked at me seriously without any expression on his dark face and twisted the point of his beard with

thumb and forefinger. My thin cotton robe was oppres-
sively warm. I smiled, hoping it was ingratiating enough to
please the doctor. Like all doctors, I knew, he didn't have a
sense of humor.

"I really want to cooperate with you, Doctor," I said
meekly, "but I actually can't see anything in those ink blots.
I'm an artist, or at least I used to be, and as an artist I can
see anything I want to see in anything."

"That's quite all right, Jordan," he said quietly. "There are
other tests." When he got to his feet I noticed he was slightly
humpbacked and I had a strong desire to rub his hump for
good luck. "Come on with me." I followed him down the
hall, Hank trailing us behind. We entered another small
room that was furnished with a small folding table, typing
paper and a battered, standard Underwood typewriter.

"Do you know how to typewrite, Jordan?" The doctor
asked me.

"Some. I haven't typed since I left high school though."

"Sit down."

I sat down at the folding table and the doctor left the
room. Hank lit a cigarette for me and before I finished it the
doctor was back with another stack of cards. These were
about eight by ten inches. He put the stack on the table and
picked up the first card to show it to me. "You'll have fun
with these."

The first picture was a reproduction of an oil painting in
black and white. It was a portrait of a young boy in white
blouse and black knickers. His hair was long, with a Dutch
bob, and he had a delicate, wistful face. He held a book in
his hand. From the side of the portrait a large hand reached
out from an unseen body and rested lightly on the boy's
shoulder. The background was an ordinary living room
with ordinary, old-fashioned furniture. Table, chairs, potted
plants and two vases full of flowers made the picture a bit
cluttered.

"What I want you to do is this:" Dr. Fischbach explained,
"Examine each picture carefully and then write a little story
about it. Anything at all, but write a story. You've got
plenty of paper and all the time in the world. After you finish with each one, put the story and picture together and
start on the next one. Number the story at the top with the

same number the picture has and they won't get mixed up. Any questions?"

"No, but I'm not much of a story teller. I don't hardly know the difference between syntax and grammar."

"Don't let that bother you. I'm not looking for polished prose, I merely want to read the stories. Get started now, and if you want to smoke, Hank'll be right outside the door to give you a light. Right, Hank?"

"Yes, sir," Hank replied with his customary smile.

They left the room and I examined the little print for a while and then put a piece of paper into the machine. It wasn't fun, as Dr. Fischbach had suggested, but it passed the time away and I would rather have something to do, anything, rather than sit in the bleak cell they had assigned me. I wrote that the young boy was sitting for his portrait and during the long period of posing he got tired and fidgety. The hand resting on his shoulder was that of his father and it was merely comforting the boy and telling him the portrait would soon be over. In a few lines I finished the dull tale.

Each picture I tackled was progressively impressionistic and it did become fun after all, once I got interested. The last three reproductions were in color, in a surrealistic vein, and they bordered on the uncanny and weird. However, I made up stories on them all, pecking them out on the old machine, even though some of the stories were quite senseless. When I finished, I racked stories and cards together and called Hank. He was down at the end of the hall talking to a nurse. He dropped the cards and stories off at the doctor's office and we started back to my cell. I stopped him.

"Just a second, Hank," I said. "Didn't you say something about a roof?"

"I don't know. We've got a roof," and he pointed toward a set of stairs leading up, right next to the elevator.

"After being cooped up so long," I said, "I'd like to get some fresh air. Do you suppose the doc would let me go up on the roof for a smoke before I go back to that little tomb? That is, if you go along."

"I'll ask him." Hank left me in the hall and entered the little office. He was smiling when he came out a moment later. "Come on," he said, taking my arm. We climbed the short flight of stairs and Hank unlocked the door to the roof.

The roof was black tar-paper, but near the little building that housed the elevator machinery and short stairwell to the sixth floor, there were about twenty feet of duckboards scattered around and a small green bench. It was late in the afternoon and a little chilly that high above the ground, but we sat and smoked on the bench for about an hour. Hank didn't mind sitting up there with me, because, as he said, if he was sitting around he wasn't working. He was an interesting man to talk to.

"How come you stay with this line of work, Hank?" I asked him.

"I drifted into it and I haven't drifted out. But it isn't as bad as it looks. There are a lot of compensations." He winked. "As a hot-shot male nurse, I rank somewhere between a doctor and an interne. I have to take orders from internes, but my pay check is about ten times as big as theirs, almost as big as some of the resident doctors. So the nurses, the lovely frustrated nurses, come flocking around, and I mean the female nurses. An interne doesn't make the dough to take them out and the doctors are married, or else they're too careful to get mixed up with fellow workers, you know, so I do all right. I get my own room right here, my meals, laundry and my money too. Funny thing about these nurses. They all look good in clean white uniforms and nice white shoes, but they look like hell when they dress up to go out. I've never known one yet who knew how to wear clothes on a date. They seem to be self-conscious about it too. But when the clothes come off, they're women, and that's the main thing with me. Did you see that nurse I was talking to in the hall?"

"I caught a glimpse of her."

"She'll be in my room tonight at eleven. So you see, Harry, taking care of nuts like you has it's compensations." He slapped me on the knee. "Come on, let's go." He laughed happily and I followed him down the stairs.

For supper that night I ate hamburger patties and boiled potatoes, lime jello and coffee. The mental work of thinking up stories had tired me and I fell asleep easily. As Hank said, having the door unlocked was almost like not being locked in.

The next morning I had another session with Dr. Fischbach. It was an easy one and didn't last very long. He gave me a written intelligence test. The questions were all fairly simple; questions like: "Who wrote *Faust?*", "How do you find the circumference of a circle?", "Who was the thirty-second president?", and so on. In the early afternoon I was given a brainwave test. It was rather painful, but interesting. After I was stretched out on a low operating table, fifty or more needles were stuck into my scalp, each needle attached with a wire to a machine. A man pushed gadgets on the machine and it made flip-flop sounds. It didn't hurt me and I didn't feel any electric shocks, but it was a little painful when the needles were inserted under the skin of my scalp. All of this procedure seemed like a great waste of time and I hated the ascetic loneliness of my wooden cell. Sleeping on the mattress without any springs made my back ache.

The next few boring days were all taken up with more tests.

X-Rays were taken of my chest, head and back.

Urine and feces specimens were taken.

More blood from my arm and from the end of my forefinger.

My eyes, ears, nose and throat were examined.

My teeth were checked.

At last I began my series of interviews with Dr. Fischbach and these were the most painful experiences of all.

flashback 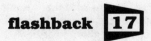 **17**

Doctor Leo Fischbach sat humped behind his desk twirling the point of his beard with thumb and forefinger. I often wondered if his beard was perfumed. It seemed to be the only link or concession between the rest of the world and his personality. If he had a personality. His large brown eyes, fixed and staring, were two dark mirrors that seemed to hold my image without interest, without curiosity, or at most, with an impersonal interest, the way one is interested in a dead, dry starfish, found on the beach. I was tense in my chair as I chain-smoked my free cigarettes and the longer I looked at Dr. Fischbach, the more I hated him. My efforts at total recollection, and he was never satisfied with less, had exhausted me. I began to speak again, my voice harsh and grating to my ears.

"The war, if anything, Doctor, was only another incident in my life. A nice long incident, but all the same, just another. I don't think it affected me at all. I was painting before I was drafted and that's all I did after I got in."

"Tell me about this, er, incident."

"Well, after I was drafted I was assigned to Fort Benning, Georgia. And after basic training I was pulled out of the group to paint murals in the mess-halls there. I was quite happy about this and I was given a free hand. Not literally, but for the army it was a good deal. Naturally, I knew the type of pictures they wanted and that's what I gave them. If I'd attempted a few non-objective pictures I'd have been handed a rifle in a hurry. So I painted army scenes. Stuff like paratroopers dropping out of the sky, a thin line of infantrymen in the field, guns, tank columns and so on."

"Did this type of thing satisfy you? Did you feel you were sacrificing your artistic principles by painting this way?"

"Not particularly. If I thought of it at all I knew I had a damned good deal. I was painting while other soldiers were drilling, running obstacle courses and getting shot at somewhere or other. I missed all that, you see. As a special duty man I was excused from everything except painting."

"You didn't paint murals for the duration of the war, did you?"

"Not at Fort Benning, no. After a year I was transferred to Camp Gordon—that's in Georgia too, at Augusta."

"What did you do there?"

"I painted murals in mess-halls."

"Didn't you have any desire for promotion?"

"No. None at all. But they promoted me anyway. I was made a T/5. Same pay as corporal but no rank or responsibilities."

"How was your reaction to the army? Did you like it?"

"I don't know."

"Did you dislike it then?"

"I don't know. I was in the army. Everybody was in the army."

"How were you treated?"

"In the army everybody is the same. Nobody bothered me, because I was on special duty. Many times the officers would come around and inspect the murals I was working on. They were well pleased, very happy about them. Knowing nothing at all about art was to their advantage. On two different occasions I was given letters of commendation for my murals. Of course, they didn't mean anything. Officers like to give letters like that; they believe it is good for morale. Maybe it is, I don't know."

"What did you do in your off-duty time in Georgia?"

Again I had to think back. What had I done? All I could remember was a blur of days, distant and hazy days. Pine trees, sand and cobalt skies. And on pay-days, gin and a girl. The rest of the month—days on a scaffolding in a hot wooden building, painting, doing the best I could with regular house paint, finishing up at the end of the day, tired but satisfied, grateful there was no sergeant to make me change what I had done. A shower, a trip to the first movie, bed by nine. Was there nothing else?

"Well, I slept a lot. It was hot in Georgia and I slept. I worked and then I hit the sack."

"When did you get discharged?"

"November, 1945. And then instead of returning to Chicago I decided to come out to California and finish art school out here."

"Why?"

"I must have forgotten to tell you about it. I had a wife and child in Chicago."

"Yes, you did." He made a note on his pad. He made his notes in a bastard mixture of loose German script and Speedwriting. "This is the first time you've mentioned a wife and child."

"It must have slipped my mind. It was some girl I married while I was attending the Chicago Art Institute. She has a child, a boy, that's right, a boy. She named him John after her father. John Jordan is his name. I've never seen him."

"Why didn't you return to your wife and child? Didn't you want to see your son? Sometimes a son is considered a great event in a man's life."

"Is that right? I considered it an unnecessary expense. I came to California because it was the practical thing to do. If I'd gone to Chicago I wouldn't have been able to continue with my painting. It would have been necessary for me to go to work and support Leonie and the child. And I didn't want to do it."

"Didn't you feel any responsibility for your wife? Or to the child?"

"Of course I did. That's why I didn't go back. I didn't want to live up to the responsibility. It was more important to paint instead. An artist paints and a husband works."

"Where's your family now?"

"I imagine they're still in Chicago. After I left the army I didn't write to her any more."

"Do you have any curiosity about how they're faring?"

"Not particularly."

Curiosity. That was an ill-chosen word for him to use. I could remember my wife well. She was a strong, intelligent, capable young woman. She thought she was a sculptor, but she had as much feeling for form as a steel worker. She didn't like Epstein and her middle-western mind couldn't grasp his purported intentions. If a statue wasn't pretty she didn't like it. But she was good on the pointing-apparatus and a fair copyist. Her drawings were rough but solid, workmanlike. She would get by, anywhere. And my son was only an accident anyway. I certainly didn't want a child, and she hadn't either. But she had one and as long as he was with his mother, as he should be, he was eating. I had no doubt about that, and no curiosity.

"And then you entered the L.A. Art Center." Dr. Fischbach prodded.

"That's right. I attended the Center for almost a year, under the G.I. Bill."

"Did you obtain a degree?"

"Just an A.A. Things didn't go so well for me after the war. I had difficulty returning to my non-objective style and

I was unable to finish any picture I started. I still can't understand it. I could visualize, to a certain extent, what my picture would look like on canvas, but I couldn't achieve it. I began and tossed aside painting after painting. The rest of my academic work was way above the average. It was easy to paint academically and I could draw as well as anybody, but that wasn't my purpose in painting."

"So you quit."

"You might say I quit. But actually, I was offered a teaching job at a private school. I weighed things over in my mind and decided to accept it. I thought I'd have more free time to paint and a place to work as an art teacher. The Center was only a place to paint and as a teacher I'd get more money than the G.I. Bill paid."

"What school did you teach at?"

"Mansfield. It's between Oceanside and San Diego. It's a rather conservative little school. There isn't much money in the endowment and the regents wouldn't accept state aid. There were about a hundred and thirty students and most of them were working their way through. It wasn't accredited under the G.I. Bill."

"How did you like teaching?"

"Painting can't be taught, Doctor. Either a man can paint or he can't. I felt that most of the students were being duped, cheated out of their money. It's one thing to study art with money furnished by a grateful government, but it's something else to pay out of your own pocket for something you aren't getting. And every day I was more convinced that I wasn't a painter and never would be one. After a while I quit painting altogether. But I hung onto my job at Mansfield because I didn't know what else to do with myself. Without art as an emotional outlet I turned to drinking as a substitute and I've been drinking ever since."

"Why did you leave Mansfield then?"

"I was fired. After I started to drink I missed a lot of classes. And I never offered any excuses when I didn't show up. In my spare time I talked to some of the more inept students and persuaded them to quit painting and go into something else. Somehow, the school didn't like that. But I was only being honest. I was merely balancing the praise I gave to the students who were good."

"After you were fired, did you come directly to San Francisco?"

"Not directly. It kind of took me by surprise, getting fired, I mean. They thought they had every reason to fire me, but I didn't expect it. I was one of the most popular teachers at the school, that is, with the students. But I suppose drinking had dulled my rational mind to the situation."

"And you felt persecuted?"

"Oh, no, nothing like that. After I got my terminal pay I thought things out. I wanted to get away from the city and things connected with culture, back to the land. Well, not back to it, because I'd never been a farmer or field hand, always in cities you know. But at the time I felt if I could work in the open using my muscles, doing really hard labor, I'd be able to sleep again. So that's what I did. I picked grapes in Fresno, and around Merced. I hit the sugar beet harvests in Chico, drifted in season, over to Utah, and I spent an entire summer in the Soledad lettuce fields."

"Were you happier doing that type of work?"

"I was completely miserable. All my life I had only wanted to paint. There isn't any substitute for painting. Coming to a sudden, brutal stop left me without anything to look forward to. I had nothing. I drank more and more and finally I couldn't hold a field hand's job, not even in the lettuce fields. That's when I came to San Francisco. It was a city and it was close. In a city a man can always live."

"And you've been here ever since?"

"That's right. I've gone from job to job, drinking when I've had the money, working for more when I ran out."

I dropped my head and sat quietly, my hands inert in my lap. I was drained. What possible good did it do the doctor to know these things about me? How could this refugee from Aachen analyze my actions for the drifting into noth-ingness when I didn't know myself? I was bored with my dull life. I didn't want to remember anything; all I wanted was peace and quiet. The silence that Death brings, an all-enveloping white cloak of everlasting darkness. By my withdrawal from the world I had made my own little niche and it was a dreary little place I didn't want to live in or tell about. But so was Doctor Fischbach's and his world was worse than mine. I wouldn't have traded places with him for anything. He sat across from me silently, fiddling with his idiotic beard, his dark eyes on the ceiling, evaluating my story, probing with his trained mind. I pitied him. The poor bastard thought he was a god.

Did I? This nasty thought hit me below the belt. How else could I have taken Helen's life if I didn't think so? What other justification was there for my brutal murder? I had no right or reason to take her with me into my nothingness. Harry Jordan had played the part of God too. It didn't matter that she had wanted to go with me. I still didn't have the right to kill her. But I had killed her and I had done it as though it was my right, merely because I loved her. Well, it was done now. No use brooding about it. At least I had done it unconsciously and I had been under the influence of gin. Doctor Fischbach was a different case. He was playing god deliberately. This strange, bearded individual had gone to medical school for years, deliberately studied psychiatry for another couple of years. He had been psychoanalyzed himself by some other foreigner who thought he was a god—and now satisfied, with an ego as large as Canada he sat behind a desk digging for filth into other people's minds. What a miserable bastard he must be behind his implacable beard and face!

"During your employment as a field hand, Jordan, did you have any periods which you felt highly elated, followed by acute depression?"

"No," I said sulledly.

"Did you ever hear voices in the night, a voice talking to you?"

"No."

"As you go about the city; have you ever had the feeling you were being followed?"

"Only once. A man followed me with a gun in his hand, but he didn't shoot me."

"You saw this man with the gun?"

"That's right, but when I looked over my shoulder he was gone."

He made some rapid, scribbling notes on his pad.

"Did you ever see him again?"

"No."

"So far, you've been reluctant to tell me about your sexual relations with Mrs. Meredith. I need this information. It's important that I know about it."

"Not to me it isn't."

"I can't see why you object to telling me about it."

"Naturally, you can't. You think you're above human relationship. To tell you about my intimate life with Helen is indecent. She's dead now, and I have too much respect for her."

"Suppose we talk then about other women in your life. Your wife, for instance. You don't seem to have any attachment for her, of any great strength. Did you enjoy a normal marital relationship?"

"I always enjoy it, but not half as much as you do second-hand."

"How do you mean that?"

I got to my feet. "I'd like to go back to my cell, Doctor," I said, forcing the words through my compressed lips. "I don't feel like talking any more."

"Very well, Jordan. We'll talk some more tomorrow."

"I'd rather not."

"Why not?"

"I don't like to waste the time. I'm not crazy and you know it as well as I do. And I resent your vicarious enjoyment of my life's history and your dirty probing mind."

"You don't really think I enjoy this, Jordan?" he said with surprise.

"You must. If you didn't you'd go into some other kind of work. I can't believe anybody would sink so low just for money. I've gone down the ladder myself, but I haven't hit your level yet."

"I'm trying to help you, Jordan."

"You can help somebody that needs it then. I don't want your help." I turned abruptly and left his office. Hank got up from the bench outside the door and accompanied me to my cell.

My cell didn't frighten me any longer. It was a haven, an escape from Dr. Fischbach. I liked its bareness, the hard mattress on the floor. It no longer mattered that I didn't have a chair to sit down upon. After a while I forced my churning mind into pleasant, happier channels. I wondered what they would have for supper.

I was hungry as hell.

the big fixation 18

When I was about seven or eight years old, somebody gave me a map of the United States that was cut up into a jigsaw puzzle. Whether I could read or not at the time I don't remember, but I had sense enough to start with the water surrounding the United States. These were the pieces with the square edges and I realized if I got the outline all around I could build toward the center a state at a time. This is the way I worked it and when I came to Kansas it was the last piece and it fitted into the center in the last remaining space. This was using my native intelligence and it was the logical method to put a jigsaw puzzle together. Evidently, Doctor Fischbach did not possess my native intelligence. He skipped around with his questions as he daily dug for more revelations from my past and he reminded me of a door-to-door salesman avoiding the houses with the BEWARE OF THE DOG signs. Having started with my relationship with Helen, dropping back to my art school days, returning to my childhood, then back to Helen, we were back to my childhood again. I no longer looked him in the eyes as we talked together, but focused my eyes on my hands or on the floor. I didn't want to let him see the hate in my eyes.

"Did your mother love you?" He asked me. "Did you feel that you got all of the attention you had coming to you?"

"Considering the fact that I had two brothers and five sisters I got my share. More than I deserved anyway, and I'm not counting two other brothers that were stillborn."

"Did you feel left out in any way?"

"Left out of what?"

"Outside of the family. Were you always fairly treated?"

"Well, Doctor, money was always short during the depression, naturally, what with the large family and all, but I always got my share. More, if anything. My father showed partiality to me; I know that now. He thought I was more gifted than my brothers and sisters."

"How did your father support the family? What type of work did he do? Was he a professional man?"

"No. He didn't have a profession, not even a trade. He contributed little, if anything, to our support. He worked once in a while, but never steady. He always said that his boss, whoever it happened to be at the time, was giving him the dirty end of the stick. He had a very strong sense of justice and he'd quit his job at the first sign of what he termed unfairness or prejudice. Even though the unfairness happened to someone else, he'd quit in protest."

"How about drinking? Did your father drink?"

"I don't know."

"Please try to remember. There might be some incidents. Surely you know whether he drank or not."

"Listen, Doctor, it was still prohibition when he was alive. I don't remember ever seeing him take a drink. And when he went out at night I was too small to go with him. So if he drank I don't know about it."

"If he didn't support your family, who did?"

"Mother. She was a beauty operator and she must have been a good one, because she always had a job. Ever since I can remember. She had some kind of a new system, and women used to come to our house on Sundays, her off-day, for treatments. It seemed to me that she never had any free time."

"What are your brothers and sisters doing now?"

"I suppose they're working. Father died first and then about a year later my mother died. From that time on we were on our own."

"How old were you then, when your mother died?"

"Sixteen."

"Weren't there any relatives to take you in with them?"

"We had relatives, yes. My mother's brother, Uncle Ralph, gathered us all together in his house about a week after her funeral. He had the insurance money by that time and it was divided equally between us. My share was two hundred and fifty dollars, which was quite a fortune in the depression. My uncle and aunt took my smallest sister to live with them, probably to get her two-fifty, but the rest of us were on our own. I got a room on the South Side, a part time job, and finished high school. I entered the Art Institute as soon as I finished high school. Luckily, I was able to snag a razor-blade-and-condom concession and this supported me and paid my tuition. I studied at the institute until I was drafted, and I've told you about my experiences in the army already."

"Sketchily."

"I told you all I could remember. I wasn't a hero. I was an ordinary soldier like all the draftees. I had a pretty good break, yes, but that was only because I had the skill to paint and also because the army gave me the opportunity to use my skill. Many other soldiers, a hell of a lot more talented than I was, were never given the same breaks."

"Do you have any desire to see your brothers and sisters again?"

"They all live in Chicago, Doctor. We used to have a saying when we were students in L.A.— 'A lousy artist doesn't go to heaven or hell when he dies; his soul goes to Chicago.' If that saying turns out to be true, I'll be seeing them soon enough."

"How about sex experiences? Did you ever engage in sex-play with your brothers and sisters?" His well-trained words marched like slugs into the cemetery of my brain. He asked this monstrous question as casually as he asked them all. Appalled, I stared at him unbelievingly.

"You must have a hell of a lot of guts to ask me a filthy question like that!" I said angrily. "What kind of a person do you think I am, anyway? I've confessed to a brutal murder—I'm guilty—I've said I was guilty! Why don't you kill me? Why can't I go to the gas chamber? What you've been doing to me can be classified as cruel and inhuman treatment, and as a citizen I don't have to take it! How much do you think I can stand?" I was on my feet by this time and pounding the doctor's desk with my fists. "You've got everything out of me you're going to get!" I finished decisively. "From now on I'll tell you nothing!"

"What is it you don't want to tell me, Jordan?" He asked

quietly, as he calmly twisted the point of his beard.

"Nothing. I've told you everything that ever happened to me. Not once, but time and time again. Why do you insist in asking the same things over and over?"

"Please sit down, Jordan." I sat down. "The reason I ask you these questions is because I haven't much time. I have to return you to the jail tomorrow—"

"Thank God for small favors!" I cut him off.

"So I've taken some unethical short cuts. I know it's most unfair to you and I'm sorry. Now. Tell me about your sex-play with your brothers and sisters."

"My brothers and I all married each other and all my sisters are lesbians. We all slept together in the same bed, including my mother and father and all of us took turns with each other. The relationship was so complicated and the experiences were so varied, all you have to do is attach a medical book of abnormal sex deviations to my file and you'll have it all. Does that satisfy your morbid curiosity?" This falsehood made me feel ashamed.

"You're evading my question. Why? Everything you tell me is strictly confidential. I only ask you these things to enable me to give a correct report—"

"From now on I'm evading you," I said. I got up from my chair and opened the door. Hank, as usual, was waiting for me outside, sitting on the bench. As I started briskly, happily, toward my cell Hank fell in behind me. My mind was relieved, my step was airy, because I never intended to talk to Dr. Fischbach again. I didn't look back and I've never seen the doctor since.

That afternoon I was so ashamed of myself and so irritable I slammed my fists into the pine wall over and over again. I kept it up until my knuckles hurt me badly enough to get my mind on them instead of the other thoughts that boiled and churned inside my head. After a while, Hank opened the door and looked in on me. There was a wide smile on his lips.

"There's a lot of noise in here. What's going on, Harry?"

"It's that damned doctor, Hank," I said. I smiled in spite of myself. Hank had the most infectious smile I've ever seen.

"Let me tell you something, Harry," Hank said seriously,

and he came as close to not smiling as he was able to do, "you've got to keep a cool stool. It don't go for a man to get emotionally disturbed in a place like this. Speaking for myself, I'll tell you this much; you'll be one hell of a lot better off in the gas chamber than you'd ever be in a state institution. Have you ever thought of that?"

I snorted. "Of course I've thought of it. But I'm not insane. You know it and so does the doctor."

"That's right, Harry. But besides working here, I've worked in three different state institutions. And I've seen guys a hell of a lot saner than you in all three of them." This remark made him laugh.

"I'm all right," I told him.

"The way to prove it is to keep a cool stool."

"I guess you're right. Doctor Fischbach says I can go back to jail tomorrow. And if he's halfway fair he'll turn in a favorable report on me, Hank. Up till today, anyway, I've cooperated with him all the way."

"I know you have, Harry. Don't spoil it. It must be pretty rough, isn't it?"

"I've never had it any rougher."

He winked at me conspiratorily. "How'd you like to have a drink?" He held up his thumb and forefinger an inch apart.

"Man, I'd love one," I replied sincerely.

Hank reached into his hip-pocket and brought out a half-pint of gin. He unscrewed the cap and offered me the bottle. I didn't take it. Was this some kind of trap? After all, Hank was a hospital employee, when all was said and done. Sure, he bad been more than nice to me so far, but maybe there had been a purpose to it, and this might be it. How did I know it was gin in the bottle? It might be some kind of dope, maybe a truth serum of some kind? It might possibly be Fischbach's way of getting me into some kind of a jam. I knew he didn't like me.

"No thanks, Hank," I said. "Maybe I'd better not."

Hank shrugged indifferently. "Suit yourself." He took a long swig, screwed the cap back on and returned the bottle to his hip pocket. He left my cell and slammed and locked the door. I was sorry I hadn't taken the drink. It might have made me feel better, and by refusing, I had hurt Hank's feelings. But it didn't make any difference. My problems were almost over. Tomorrow I would be back in jail. It would be almost like going home again.

That night I couldn't sleep. After twisting and turning on the uncomfortable mattress until eleven, I gave up the battle and banged on the door for the nurse. The night nurse gave me a sleeping pill without any argument, but even then it was a long time before I got to sleep. The next morning Hank brought me my breakfast on a tray. If he was still sore at me he didn't give any indication of it.

"This'll be your last meal here, Harry," he said, smiling.

"That's the best news I've had since I got here," I said. "Hank, I'm really sorry about not taking that drink you offered me yesterday. I was upset, nervous, and—"

"It doesn't bother me, Harry. I just thought you'd like a little shot."

"After a man's been in this place a while, he gets so he doesn't trust anybody."

"You're telling me!" He opened the door and looked down the corridor, turned and smiled broadly. "I found out something for you, Harry. Last night I managed to get a look at your chart, and Doctor Fischbach is reporting you as absolutely sane. In his report he stated that you were completely in possession of your faculties when you croaked your girl friend."

"That's really good news. Maybe Doctor Fischbach's got a few human qualities after all."

"I thought it would make you happy," Hank said pleasantly.

"What about the Sanity Board you were telling me about the other day? Won't I have to meet that?"

"Not as long as Fischbach says your okay. He classified you as neurotic depressive, which doesn't mean a damn thing. The Sanity Board is for those guys who have a reasonable doubt. You're all right."

I tore into my breakfast with satisfaction. Now I could go back to the special block safe in the knowledge I would go to the gas chamber instead of the asylum. Hank was in a talkative mood and he chatted about hospital politics while I finished my breakfast, brought me another cup of coffee when I asked for it.

"Now that I'm leaving, Hank," I said "tell me something. Why is it that I never get a hot cup of coffee? This is barely lukewarm."

He laughed. "I never give patients hot coffee. About two years ago I was taking a pot of hot coffee around the ward giving refills and I asked this guy if he wanted a second cup. 'No,' he says, so I said, 'Not even a half a cup?' and he says, 'Okay.' So I pours about a half-cup and he says, 'A little more.' I pours a little more, and he says, 'More yet.' This time I filled his cup all the way. He reached out then, grabbed my waistband and dumped the whole cupful of hot coffee inside my pants! Liked to have ruined me. I was in bed for three days with second degree burns!"

I joined Hank in laughter, not because it was a funny story, but he told it so well. He finished with the punch line:

"Ever since then I've never given out with hot coffee."

Hank lit my cigarette and we shook hands. He picked up my tray.

"I want to wish you the best of luck Harry," he said at the door. "You're one of the nicest guys we've had in here in a long time."

"The same goes for you, Hank," I said sincerely. "You've made it bearable for me and I want you to know I appreciate it."

More than a little embarrassed, he turned away with the tray and walked out, leaving the door open. Smitty, another orderly, brought me my clothes and I changed into them quickly. Smitty unlocked the elevator and we rode down to the receiving entrance and I was turned over to a detective in a dark gray suit. I was handcuffed and returned to the jail in a police car instead of an ambulance. I was signed in at the jail and Mr. Benson returned me to my cell, my old cell.

Wearing my blue jail clothes again and stretched out on my bunk, I sighed with contentment. I speculated on how long it would be before the trial. It couldn't be too long, now that the returns were in; all I needed now, I supposed, was an open date on the court calendar. If I could occupy myself somehow, it would make the time pass faster. Maybe, if I asked Mr. Benson, he would get me a drawing pad and some charcoal sticks. I could do a few sketches to pass away the time. It was a better pastime than reading and it would be something to do.

That afternoon, right after lunch, I talked to Mr. Benson, and he said he would see what he could do . . .

portrait of a killer 19

It must have been about an hour after breakfast. The daily breakfast of two thick slices of bread and the big cup of black coffee didn't always set so well. Scrambled eggs, toast, and a glass of orange juice would have been better. No question about it; I had eaten better at the hospital. The two lumps of dough had absorbed the coffee and the mess felt like a full sponge in my stomach. Somebody was at my door and I looked up. It was Mr. Benson. He had a large drawing pad and a box of colored pencils in his hand. The old man was smiling and it revealed his worn down teeth, uppers and lowers. He stopped smiling the moment I looked at him.

"I bought you this stuff outa my own pocket," he said gruffly. "You can't lay around in here forever doin' nothin'." He passed the pad and pencil box through the bars and I took them.

"Thanks a lot, Mr. Benson," I said. "How'd you think to have me do your portrait? That is, after I practice up a little."

"You pretty good?"

"I used to be, and you've got an interesting face."

"What do you mean by that!" He bridled.

"I mean I'd enjoy trying to draw you."

"Oh." His face flushed. "I guess I wouldn't mind you doin' a picture of me. Maybe some time this afternoon?"

"Any time."

I practiced and experimented with the colored pencils all morning, drawing cones, blocks, trying for perspective. I would rather have had charcoal instead of colored pencils, I like it much better, but maybe the colored pencils gave me

more things to do. The morning passed like a shot. I hadn't
lost my touch, if anything, my hand was steadier than it
had been before.

Mr. Benson held out until mid-afternoon, and then he
brought a stool down the corridor and seated himself outside my cell. For some reason, a portrait, whether a plain
drawing or a full-scale painting, is the most flattering thing
you can do for a person. I've never met a person yet who
didn't want an artist to paint his portrait. It is one of the
holdovers from the nineteenth century that enables artists
who go for that sort of thing to eat. A simple drawing, or a
painting should always be done from life to be worthwhile.
But this doesn't prevent an organization in New York from
making thousands of dollars weekly by having well-known
artists paint portraits from photographs that are sent in
from all over the United States. If the person has enough
money, all he has to do is state what artist he wants and
send in his photographs. The artists who do this type of
work are a hell of a lot hungrier for money than I ever was.

I didn't spend much time with Mr. Benson. I did a profile
view and by doing a profile it is almost impossible not to get
a good likeness. By using black, coral, and a white pencil
for the highlights, I got the little drawing turned out well
and Mr. Benson was more than pleased.

"What do I owe you, Harry?" he asked, after I tore the
drawing from the pad and gave it to him.

"Nothing." I laughed. "You're helping me kill time, and
besides you bought me the pad and pencils."

"How about a dollar?"

"No." I shook my head. "Nothing."

"Suit yourself." He picked up his stool and left happily
with his picture.

Mr. Benson must have spread the word or showed his
picture around. In the next three days I did several more
drawings. Detectives came up to see me and they would sit
belligerently, trying to cover their embarrassment while I
whipped out a fast profile. They all offered me money,
which I didn't accept, but I never refused a pack of cigarettes. The last portrait I did was that of a young girl. She
was one of the stenos from the filing department, well-liked
by Mr. Benson, and he let her in. She was very nervous and

twitched on the stool while I did a three-quarter view. I suppose she was curious to see what I looked like, more than anything else, but it didn't matter to me. Drawing was a time-killer to me. I gave her the completed drawing and she hesitated outside my cell.

"You haven't been reading the papers have you, ah, Mr. Jordan?" she asked nervously.

"No."

She was about twenty-one or -two with thin blonde hair, glasses, and a green faille suit. Her figure was slim, almost slight, and she twisted her long, slender fingers nervously. "I don't know whether to tell you or not, but seeing you don't read the papers, maybe I'd better . . ."

"Tell me what?" I asked gently.

"Oh, it just makes me sore, that's all!" She said spiritedly. "These detectives! Here you've been decent enough to draw their pictures for nothing, and they've been selling them to the newshawks in the building. All of the papers have been running cuts, and these detectives have been getting ten dollars or more from the reporters."

"The reporters have been getting gypped then," I said, controlling my sudden anger.

"Well I think it's dirty, Mr. Jordan, and I just wanted you to know that I'm going to keep my picture."

"That's fine. Just tell Mr. Benson I'm not doing any more portraits. Tell him on your way out, will you please?"

"All right. Don't tell anybody I told you . . . huh?"

"No, I won't say anything. I'm not sore about them selling the pictures," I told her. "It's just that they aren't good enough for publication."

"*I* think they are." She gave me two packages of Camels and tripped away down the corridor. At first I was angry and then I had to laugh at the irony of the situation. Ten dollars. Nobody had ever paid me ten dollars for a picture. Of course, I had never priced a painting that low. The few I had exhibited, in the Chicago student shows, had all been priced at three hundred or more dollars, and none of then had sold. But anyway, no more portraits from Harry Jordan. The cheap Harry Jordan integrity would be upheld until the last sniff of cyanide gas. . . . Again I laughed.

The following afternoon, Mr. Benson opened the cell

door and beckoned to me. He led me through a couple of corridors and into a small room sparsely furnished with a bare scratched desk, a couple of wooden chairs and, surprisingly, a leather couch without arms, but hinged at one end so that the head of it could be raised. It was the kind of a couch you sometimes see in psychiatrists' offices and doctors' examining rooms. "What's this?" I said.

"Examining room," he said, as I'd expected. I started to get angry. He left the room, moving rather furtively, I thought, and he shut the door, locking it on the outside. After a couple of minutes the door opened again. It was that stenographer.

She walked in, her arms full of the drawing stuff I had left in my cell. The door closed behind her and I heard the lock click again, shutting us in. I couldn't figure it out.

She was looking at me, kind of breathlessly. She put the colored pencils and stuff down on the desk. "I want you to draw me again," she said.

"I don't know as I want to do any more drawing."

"Please."

"Why in here?"

"You don't understand. I want you to draw me in the nude."

I looked at her. It was warm in the room, and there was plenty of light streaming in from the high, barred windows. The bars threw interesting shadows across her body. It was a good place to draw or paint, all right. But that wasn't what she wanted. I knew that much.

I sat woodenly. She laughed, kicked off her shoes, lay back on the couch. I could tell she was a little scared of me, but liking it. "I'll be pretty in the nude," she said. "I'll be wonderful to draw." She lifted a long and delicately formed leg and drew off the stocking. She did the same for her other leg. I could see that her thighs were a trifle plump. They were creamy-white, soft-looking, but the rest of her legs, especially around the knees, were faintly rosy.

She flicked a glance at me, to see what my response was. I had not moved. I was just standing there, watching. She stood up, made an eager, ungraceful gesture that unloosed a clasp, or a zipper or something. Her skimpy green skirt fell to the floor. She hesitated then, like a girl about to

plunge into a cold shower, but took a deep breath, then
quickly undid her blouse. It fell to the floor with the skirt.
Another moment and her slip was off, and the wisps of
nylon that were her underthings. I smelled their faint perfume in the warm room. She lifted her arms over her head
and pirouetted proudly. "See?" she said. "See?"

I had not noticed before, even when I had been drawing
her, how pretty she was. Maybe she was the kind of girl
whose beauty only awakes when her clothes are off. I
examined her thoughtfully, trying to think of her as a prob-
lem in art. Long legs. Plump around the hips and thighs.
Narrow, long waist. Jutting bosom, a trifle too soft, too
immature. Her face was narrow and bony, but attractive
enough. The lips were full and red. Her corn-colored hair
fell in a graceful line to her shoulders.

"You fixed this up?" I said.

She was tense and excited. "Me and Mr. Benson," she
said. "Nobody will bother us here." She giggled.

This would be the last time, I was thinking. I would never
have another chance at a woman. Not on this earth.

"Don't look so surprised," she said. "All kinds of things
go on in a place like this. It's just a question of how much
money and influence a person has. You don't have money,
and neither do I—but I've got the influence—" She giggled
again. Like a high school kid. Was this her first adventure
with a man, I wondered.

I sat down on the hard leather couch.

"Come here," I said.

She sat down on my lap.

I started by kissing her. First her silky hair. Then her soft
parted lips. Then her neck, her shoulders, lower . . .

"Harry," she said. "Harry!"

My arm was around her waist, and her skin felt creamy
and smooth. I tilted her back, swinging her off my knees so
that she lay supine on the couch. I stroked and kissed and
fondled, slowly and easily at first, then faster and harder.
Much harder. She began to breathe deeply. She was scared.
I kissed her neck, at the same time taking her by the hair
and drawing her head back.

"Harry," she said. "What are you going to do to me?"

"You're frightened, aren't you? That's part of the thrill.

That's what you want, isn't it? To do it with a freak. A dangerous freak. And a murderer!"

"I want you, Harry!"

She was panting. She threw her arms around me, and her nails clawed my shoulders. It was my head that was pulled down now, and she was smothering me with lipstick and feverish kisses. This was the moment I had been waiting for. The moment when she would be craving ecstasy. I lifted my hand and, as hard as I could, slapped her in the face.

But instead of looking at me with consternation and fear and disappointment, she giggled. Damn her, in her eyes I was just living up to expectations. This was what she had come for!

In cold disgust, I hit her with my fist, splitting her lip so that the blood ran. The blow rolled her from the couch to the floor. For a moment I pitied her bare, crumpled body, but as soon as the breath got back into her she sprang to her feet. I was standing now, too. She flung her arms around me in a desperate embrace. "I can't bear it. Please, Harry!"

I knocked her down again.

"Please, Harry! Now . . . Now . . . !"

"You slut. I loved a real woman. To her, I was no strange, freakish creature. She didn't come to me for cheap thrills. Get your clothes on!"

I picked up one of the chairs and swung at the door with it.

"Let me out of here," I shouted, pounding the door. "God damn it, let me out!"

Mr. Benson came, and shamefacedly opened the door. The girl, her clothes on, ran sobbing down the corridor. Mr. Benson looked at me.

"I'm sorry, Harry. I thought I was doing you a favor."

I never did find out the girl's name.

The next day was Sunday. After a heavy lunch of baked swordfish and boiled potatoes I fell asleep on my bunk for a little afternoon nap. The jailer aroused me by reaching through the bars and jerking on my foot. It wasn't Mr. Benson; it was the Sunday man, Mr. Paige.

"Come on, Jordan," he said, "wake up. You gotta visitor."

Mr. Paige sold men's suits during the week, but he was a member of the Police Reserve, and managed to pick up extra money during the month by getting an active duty day of pay for Sunday work. At least, that is what Mr. Benson told me.

"I'm too sleepy for visitors," I grumbled, still partly asleep. "Who is it anyway?"

"It's a woman," he said softly, "a Mrs. Mathews." I could tell by the expression on his face and his tone of voice he knew Mrs. Mathews was Helen's mother. "Do you want to see her?"

I got off the bed in a hurry. No. Of course I didn't want to see her. But that wasn't the point. She wanted to see me and I couldn't very well refuse. She had every right to see the murderer of her daughter.

"Do you know what she wants to see me about?" I asked Mr. Paige.

He shook his head. "All I know, she's got a pass from the D.A. Even so, if you don't want, you don't have to talk to her."

"I guess it's all right. Give me a light." He lit my cigarette for me and I took several fast drags, hoping the smoke would dissipate my drowsiness. Smoking, I stood close to the barred door, listening nervously for the sound of Mrs. Mathews' footsteps in the corridor. And I heard her long before I saw her. Her step was strong, resolute, purposeful. And she appeared in front of the door, Mr. Paige, the jailer, behind her and slightly to one side.

"Here's Harry Jordan, ma'am. You can't go inside the cell, but you can talk to him for five minutes." I was grateful for the time limit Mr. Paige arbitrarily imposed. He turned away, walked a few steps down the corridor, out of earshot, beyond my range of vision.

Mrs. Mathews was wearing that same beaver coat, black walking shoes, and a green felt, off-the-face hat. Her gray hair was gathered and piled in a knot on the back of her neck. She glared at me through her gold-rimmed glasses. Her full lips curled back, showing her teeth, in a scornful, sneering grimace of disgust. There was a bright gleam of hatred in her eyes, the unreasoning kind of hate one reserves for a dangerous animal, or a loose snake. She made me extremely nervous, looking at me that way. My hands were damp and I took them away from the bars, wiped my palms on my shirt. As tightly as I could, I gripped the bars again.

"It was nice of you to come and visit me, Mrs. Mathews . . ." I said haltingly. She didn't reply to my opening remark and I didn't know what else to say. But I tried.

"I'm sorry things turned out the way they did," I said humbly, "but I want you to know that Helen was in full accord with what I did. It was the way Helen wanted it . . ." My throat was tight, like somebody was holding my windpipe, and I had to force the words out of my mouth. "If we had it all to do over again, maybe things would have worked out differently . . ."

Mrs. Mathews worked her mouth in and out, pursed her lips.

"I've pleaded guilty, and—" I didn't get to finish my sentence.

Without warning, Mrs. Mathews spat into my face. Involuntarily, I jerked back from the bars. Ordinarily, a woman is quite awkward when she tries to spit. Mrs. Mathews was not. The wet, disgusting spittle struck my forehead, right above my eyebrows. I made no attempt to wipe it off, but came forward again, and tightly gripped the bars. I waited patiently for a stream of invective to follow, but it didn't come. Mrs. Mathews glared at me for another long moment, sniffed, jerked her head to the right, turned and lumbered away.

I sat down on my bunk, wiped off my face with the back of my hand. My legs and hands were trembling and I was as weak as if I had climbed out of a hot Turkish bath.

My mind didn't function very well. Maybe I had it coming to me. At least in her eyes, I did. I didn't know what to think. The viciousness and sudden fury of her pointless action had taken me completely by surprise. But how many times must I be punished before I was put to death? I don't believe I was angry, not even bitter. There was a certain turmoil inside my chest, but it was caused mostly by my reaction to her intense hatred of me. In addition to my disgust and loathing for the woman I also managed to feel sorry for her and I suspected she would suffer later for her impulsive action. After she reflected, perhaps shame would come and she would regret her impulsiveness. It was like kicking an unconscious man in the face. But on the other hand, she had probably planned what she would do for several days. I didn't want to think about it. Mr. Paige was outside the door and there was a contrite expression on his face.

"She didn't stay long," he said.

"No. She didn't."

"I saw what she did," Mr. Paige said indignantly. "If I'd have known what she was up to I wouldn't have let her in, even if she did have a pass from the D.A."

"That's all right, Mr. Paige. I don't blame you; I don't blame anybody. But if she comes back, don't let her in again. I don't want to see her any more. My life is too short."

"Don't worry, Jordan. She won't get in again!" He said this positively. He walked away and I was alone. I washed my face with the brown soap and cold water in my wash basin a dozen times, but my face still felt dirty.

The next day my appetite was off. I tried to draw something, anything, to pass the time away, but I couldn't keep my mind on it. Mr. Paige had told Mr. Benson what had happened and he had tried to talk to me about it, and I cut him off quickly. I didn't feel like talking. I lay on my back all day long, smoking cigarettes, one after another, and looking at the ceiling.

On Tuesday, I had another visitor. Mr. Benson appeared outside my cell with a well-fed man wearing a brown gabardine Brooks Brothers suit and a blue satin vest. His face was lobster red and his larynx gave him trouble when he talked. Mr. Benson opened the door and let the man into my cell.

"This is Mr. Dorrell, Jordan," the old jailer said. "He's an editor from *He-Men Magazine* and he's got an okay from the D.A.'s office so I gotta let him in for ten minutes."

"All right," I said, and I didn't move from my reclining position. There were no stools or chairs and Mr. Dorrell had to stand. "What can I do for you, Mr Dorrell?" I asked.

"I'm from *He-Men*, Mr. Jordan," he began in his throaty voice. "And our entire editorial staff is interested in your case. To get directly to the point—we want an 'as-told-to' story from you, starting right at the beginning of your, ah, relationship with Mrs. Meredith."

"No. That's impossible."

"No," he smiled, "it isn't impossible. There is a lot of interest for people when a woman as prominent in society as Mrs. Meredith, gets, shall we say, involved?"

"Helen wasn't prominent in society."

"Maybe not, not as you and I know it, Mr. Jordan. But certain places, like Biarritz, for instance, Venice, and in California, San Sienna, are very romantic watering places. And the doings of their inhabitants interests our readers very much."

"My answer is no."

"We'll pay you one thousand dollars for such an article."

"I don't want a thousand dollars."

"You might need it."

"What for?"

"Money comes in handy sometimes," he croaked, "and the public has a right to know about your case."

"Why do they?" I asked belligerently. "It's nobody's business but my own!"

"Suppose you consider the offer and let us know later?"

"No. I won't even consider it. I don't blame you, Mr. Dorrell. You've got a job to do. And I suppose your readers would get a certain amount of morbid enjoyment from my unhappy plight, and possibly more copies of your magazine would be bought. But I can't allow myself to sell such a story. It's impossible."

"Well, I won't say anything more." Mr. Dorrell took a card out of his wallet and handed it to me. "If you happen to change your mind, send me a wire. Send it collect, and I'll send a feature writer to see you and he'll bring you a check, in advance."

At the door he called for Mr. Benson. The jailer let him out of the cell and locked the door again. The two of them chatted as they walked down the corridor and I tore the business card into several small pieces and threw them on the floor. If Mr. Dorrell had been disappointed by my refusal he certainly didn't show it. What kind of a world did I live in, anyway? Everybody seemed to believe that money was everything, that it could buy integrity, brains, art, and now a man's soul. I had never had a thousand dollars at one time in my entire life. And now, when I had an opportunity to have that much money, I was in a position to turn it down. It made me feel better and I derived a certain satisfaction from the fact that I could turn it down. In my present position, I could afford to turn down ten thousand, a million . . .

I didn't eat any supper that evening. After drinking the black coffee I tried to sleep but all night long I rolled and tossed on my narrow bunk. From time to time I dozed, but I always awakened with a start, and my heart would violently pound. There was a dream after me, a bad dream, and my sleeping mind wouldn't accept it. I was grateful when morning came at last. I knew it was morning, because Mr. Benson brought my breakfast.

After breakfast, when I took my daily shower, I noticed the half-smile on the old jailer's face. He gave me my razor, handing it in to me as I stood under the hot water, and not only did I get a few extra minutes in the shower, I got a better shave with the hot water. As I toweled myself I wondered what was behind the old man's smile.

"What's the joke, Mr. Benson?" I asked.

"I've got news for you, Jordan, but I don't know whether it's good or bad." His smile broadened.

"What news?"

"You're being tried today."

"It's good news."

He brought me my own clothes and I put them on, tied my necktie as carefully as I could without a mirror. I had to wait in my cell for about a half-hour and then I was handcuffed and taken down to the receiving office and checked out. My stuff was returned and I signed the envelope to show that I had gotten it back. All of it. Button, piece of string, handkerchief, and parking stub from the Continental Garage. As the detective and I started toward the parking ramp the desk seargent called out to the officer. We paused.

"He's minimum security, Jeff."

Jeff removed the handcuffs and we climbed into the waiting police car for the short drive to the Court House.

trial 20

I was in a small room adjacent to the courtroom. It was sparsely furnished; just a small chipped wooden table against the wall and four metal chairs. I stood by the window, looking down three stories at the gray haze of fog that palled down over the civic center. A middle-aged uniformed policeman was stationed in the room to stand guard over me, and he leaned against the wall by the door, picking at the loose threads of the buttonholes on his shiny Navy blue serge uniform. There was nothing much to see out of the window, only the fog, the dim outlines of automobiles with their lights on, in the street below, a few walking figures, their sex indistinguishable, but I looked out because it was a window and I hadn't been in a room with a window for a long time. One at a time I pulled at my fingers, cracking the joints. The middle finger of my left hand made the loudest crack.

"Don't do that," the policeman said. "I can't stand it. And besides, cracking your knuckles makes them swell."

I stopped popping my fingers and put my hands in my trousers pockets. That didn't feel right, so I put my hands in my jacket pockets. This was worse. I let my arms hang, swinging them back and forth like useless pendula. I didn't want to smoke because my mouth and throat were too dry, but I got a light from the policeman and inhaled the smoke into my lungs, even though it tasted like scraped bone dust. Before I finished the cigarette there was a hard rapping on the door and the policeman opened it.

A round, overweight man with a shiny bald head bounced into the room. He didn't come into the room, he "came on," like a TV master of ceremonies. There was a hearty falseness to the broad smile on his round face and his eyes were black and glittering, almost hidden by thick, sagging folds of flesh. His white hands were short, white, and puffy, and the scattering of paprika freckles made them look unhealthily pale. I almost expected him to say, "A funny thing happened to me on the way over to the court house today," but instead of saying anything he burst into a contagious, raucous, guffawing laugh that reverberated in the silence of the little room. It was the type of laughter that is usually infectious, but in my solemn frame of mind I didn't feel like joining him. After a moment he stopped abruptly, wiped his dry face with a white handkerchief.

"You are Harry Jordan!" He pointed a blunt fat finger at me.

"Yes, sir," I said.

"I'm Larry Hingen-Bergen." He unbuttoned his double-breasted tweed coat and sat down at the little table. He threw his battered briefcase on the table before him and indicated, by pointing to another chair that he wanted me to sit down. I pulled up a chair, sat down and faced him diagonally. "I'm your defense counsel, Jordan, appointed by the court. I suppose you wonder why I haven't been to see you before this?" He closed his eyes, while he waited for my answer.

"No. Not particularly, Mr. Hingen-Bergen. After I told the District Attorney I was guilty, I didn't think I'd need a defense counsel."

His eyes snapped open, glittering. "And you don't!" He guffawed loudly, with false heartiness. "And you don't!" He let the laugh loose again, slapped his heavy thigh with his hand. "You!" He pointed his finger at my nose, "are a very lucky boy! In fact," his expression sobered, "I don't know how to tell you how lucky you are. You're going to be a free man, Jordan."

"What's that?" I asked stupidly.

"Free. Here's the story." He related it in a sober, business-like manner. "I was assigned to your case about two weeks ago, Jordan. Naturally, the first thing I did was have a little talk with Mr. Seely. You remember him?"

I nodded. "The Assistant D.A."

"My visit happened to coincide with the day the medical report came in. Now get a grip on yourself, boy. Helen Meredith was not choked to death, as you claimed; she died a natural death!" He took a small notebook out of his pocket. It was a long and narrow notebook, fastened at the top, covered with green imitation snakeskin, the kind insurance salesmen give away whether you buy any insurance or not. I sat dazed, tense, leaning forward slightly while he leafed through the little book. "Here it is," he said, smiling. "Coronary thrombosis. Know what that is?"

"It isn't true!" I exclaimed.

He gripped my arm with his right hand, his voice softened. "I'm afraid it is true, Jordan. Of course, there were bruises on her neck and throat where your hands had been, but that's all they were. Bruises. She actually died from a heart attack. Did she ever tell you she had a bad heart?"

I shook my head, scarcely hearing the question. "No. No, she didn't. Her mother said something about it once, but I didn't pay much attention at the time. And I can't believe this, Mr. Hingen-Bergen. She was always real healthy; why she didn't hardly get a hangover when she drank."

"I'm not making this up, Jordan." He tapped the notebook with the back of his fat fingers. "This was the Medical Examiner's report. Right from the M.E.'s autopsy. There's no case against you at all. Now, the reason the D.A. didn't tell you about this was because he wanted to get a full psychiatrist's report first." Mr. Hingen-Bergen laughed, but it was a softer laugh, kind. "You *might* have been insane, you know. He had to find out before he could release you."

My mind still wouldn't accept the situation. "But if I didn't actually kill her, Mr. Hingen-Bergen, I must have at least hastened her death! And if so, that makes me guilty, doesn't it?"

"No," he replied flatly. "She'd have died anyway. I read the full M.E. report. She was in pretty bad shape. Malnutrition, I don't remember what all. You didn't have anything to do with her death."

The middle-aged policeman had been attentively following the conversation. "By God," he remarked, "this is an interesting case, Mr. Hingen-Bergen!"

"Isn't it?" The fat lawyer smiled at him. He turned to me again. "Now, Jordan, we're going into the court room and Mr. Seely will present the facts to the judge. He'll move for a dismissal of the charges and you'll be free to go."

"Go where?" My mind was in a turmoil.

"Why, anywhere you want to go, naturally. You'll be a free man! Why, this is the easiest case I've ever had. Usually my clients go to jail!" He laughed boisterously and the policeman joined him. "You just sit tight, Jordan, and the bailiff'll call you in a few minutes." He picked his briefcase up from the table and left the room.

I remained in my chair, my mind numb. If this was true, and evidently it was—the lawyer wouldn't lie to me right before the trial—I hadn't done anything! Not only had I fumbled my own suicide, I'd fumbled Helen's death too. I could remember the scene so vividly. I could remember the feel of her throat beneath my thumbs, and the anguish I had undergone . . . and all of it for nothing. Nothing. I covered my face with my hands. I felt a hand on my shoulder. It was the policeman's hand and he tried to cheer me up.

"Why, hell, boy," he said friendly, "don't take it so hard. You're lucky as hell. Here . . ." I dropped my hands to my lap. The policeman held out a package of cigarettes. "Take one." I took one and he lighted it for me. "You don't want to let this prey on your mind. You've got a chance to start your life all over again. Take it. Be grateful for it."

"It was quite a shock. I wasn't ready for it."

"So what? You're out of it, forget it. Better pull yourself together. You'll be seeing the judge pretty soon."

The bailiff and Mr. Hingen-Bergen came for me and took me into the court room. I'd never seen a regular trial before. All I knew about court room procedure was what I had seen in movies; and movie trials are highly dramatic, loud voices, screaming accusations, bawling witnesses, things like that. This was unlike anything I'd ever seen before. Mr. Hingen-Bergen and I joined the group at the long table. The judge sat at the end wearing his dark robes. And he was a young man, not too many years past thirty; he didn't look as old as Mr. Seely. Mr. Seely sat next to the judge, his face incompliant behind his glasses. It was a large room, not a regular courtroom, and there were no spectators. A male stenographer, in his early twenties, made a fifth at the table. The bailiff leaned against the door, smoking a pipe.

Mr. Seely and the judge carried on what seemed to be a friendly conversation. I didn't pay any attention to what they were saying; I was waiting for the trial to get started.

"The Medical Examiner couldn't make it, your honor," Mr. Seely said quietly to the judge, "but here's his report, if that's satisfactory."

There was a long period of silence while the judge studied the typewritten sheets. The judge slid the report across the desk to Mr. Seely, and the Assistant District Attorney put it back inside his new cowhide briefcase. The judge pursed his lips and looked at me for a moment, nodding his head up and down soberly.

"I believe you're right, Mr. Seely," he said softly. "There's really no point in holding the defendant any longer. The case is dismissed." He got to his feet, rested his knuckles on the desk and stared at me. I thought he was going to say something to me, but he didn't. He gathered his robes about him, lifting the hems clear of the floor, and Mr. Hingen-Bergen and I stood up. He left the courtroom by a side door. Mr. Seely walked around the table and shook hands with me.

"I've got some advice for you, Jordan," Mr. Seely said brusquely. "Keep away from liquor, and see if you can find another city to live in."

"Yes, sir," I said.

"That's good advice," Mr. Hingen-Bergen added.

"Of course," Mr. Seely amended gravely, "you don't *have* to leave San Francisco. Larry can tell you that." He looked sideways at my fat defense counsel. "You're free to live any place you want to, but I believe my advice is sound."

"You bet!" Mr. Hingen-Bergen agreed. "Especially, not drinking. You might end up in jail again if you go on a bat."

"Thanks a lot," I said vaguely.

I didn't know what to do with myself. Mr. Seely and the bailiff followed the young stenographer out of the room and I was still standing behind the table with Mr. Hingen-Bergen. He was stuffing some papers into various compartments of his briefcase. I had been told what to do and when to do it for so long I suppose I was waiting for somebody to tell me when to leave.

"Ready to go, Jordan?" Mr. Hingen-Bergen asked me, as he hooked the last strap on his worn leather bag.

"Don't I have to sign something?" It all seemed too unreal to me.

"Nope. That's it. You've had it."

"Then I guess I'm ready to go."

"Fine. I'll buy you a cup of coffee."

I shook my head. "No thanks. I don't believe I want one."

"Suit yourself. What are your plans?"

Again I shook my head bewilderedly. "I don't know. This thing's too much of a surprise. I still can't grasp it or accept it, much less formulate plans."

"You'll be all right." He laughed his coarse hearty laugh. "Come on."

Mr. Hingen-Bergen took my arm and we left the court room, rode the elevator down to the main floor. We stood on the marble floor of the large entrance way and he pointed to the outside door, the steep flight of stairs leading down to the street level.

"There you are, Jordan," the lawyer smiled. "The city."

I nodded, turned away and started down the steps. Because of the heavy fog I could only see a few feet ahead of me. I heard footsteps behind me and turned as Mr. Hingen-Bergen called out my name.

"Have you got any money?" the lawyer asked me kindly.

"No, sir."

"Here." He handed me a five dollar bill. "This'll help you get started maybe."

I accepted the bill, folded it, put it into my watch pocket.

"I don't know when I'll be able to pay you back . . ." I said lamely.

"Forget it! Next time you get in jail, just look me up!" He laughed boisterously, clapped me on the shoulder and puffed up the stairs into the court house.

I continued slowly down the steps and when I reached the sidewalk, turned left toward Market. I was a free man.

Or was I?

from here to eternity

After I left the Court House I walked for several blocks before I realized I was walking aimlessly and without a destination in mind. So much had happened unexpectedly I was in a daze. The ugly word, "Freedom" overlapped and crowded out any nearly rational thoughts that tried to cope with it. Freedom meant nothing to me. After the time I had spent in jail and in the hospital, not only was I reconciled to the prospect of death, I had eagerly looked forward to it. I wanted to die and I deserved to die. But I was an innocent man. I was free. I was free to wash dishes again, free to smash baggage, carry a waiter's tray, dish up chile beans as a counterman. Free.

The lights on the marquee up ahead advertised two sure-fire movies. Two old Humphrey Bogart pictures. It was the Bijou Theatre and I had reached Benny's Bijou Beanery. This was where it had started. I looked through the dirty glass of the window. Benny sat in his customary seat behind the cash register and as I watched him he reached into the large jar of orange gum drops on the counter and popped one into his mouth. The cafe was well-filled, most of the stools taken and two countermen were working behind the counter. Just to see the cafe brought back a vivid memory of Helen and the way she looked and laughed the night she first entered. I turned away and a tear escaped my right eye and rolled down my cheek. A passerby gave me a sharp look. I wiped my eyes with the back of my hand and entered the next bar I came to. Tears in a bar are not unusual.

The clock next to the mouldy deer antlers over the mirror read ten-fifty-five. Except for two soldiers and a B-girl between them, the bar was deserted. I went to the far end and sat down.

"Two ounces of gin and a slice of lemon," I told the bartender.

"No chaser?"

"Better give me a little ice water."

I was in better physical condition than I had enjoyed in two or three years, but after my layoff I expected the first drink to hit me like a sledge hammer. There was no effect. The gin rolled down my throat like a sweet cough syrup with a codeine base. I didn't need the lemon or the water.

"Give me another just like it," I said to the bartender.

After three more my numb feeling disappeared. I wasn't drunk, but my head was clear and I was able to think again. Not that it made any difference, because nothing mattered anymore. I unfolded the five dollar bill Mr. Hingen-Bergen had given me, paid for the drinks and returned to the street. There was a cable car dragging up the hill and it slowed down at my signal. I leaped aboard for the familiar ride to my old neighborhood and the roominghouse. I could no longer think of the ride as going home. Although the trip took a long while it seemed much too short. At my corner, I jumped down.

The well-remembered sign, BIG MIKE'S BAR & GRILL, the twisted red neon tubing, glowed and hummed above the double doors of the saloon. This was really my home, mine and Helen's. This was where we had spent our only really happy hours; hours of plain sitting, drinking, with our shoulders touching. Hours of looking into each other's eyes in the bar mirror. As I stood there, looking at the entrance, the image of Helen's loveliness was vivid in my mind.

Rodney, the crippled newsboy, left his pile of papers and limped toward me. There was surprise in his tired face and eyes.

"Hello Harry," he said, stretching out his arm. I shook his hand.

"Hello, Rodney."

"You got out of it, huh?"

"Yes."

"Congratulations, Harry. None of us around here really expected you—I mean, well . . ." His voice trailed off.

"That's all right, Rodney. It was all a mistake and I don't want to talk about it."

"Sure, Harry. I'm glad you aren't guilty." Self-conscious,

he bobbed his head a couple of times and returned to his newspapers. I pushed through the swinging doors and took the first empty seat at the bar. It was lunch hour and the bar and cafe were both busy; most of the stools were taken and all of the booths. As soon as he saw me, Big Mike left the cash register and waddled toward me.

"The usual, Harry?" he asked me quietly.

"No. I don't want a drink."

Mike's face was unfathomable and I didn't know how he would take the news.

"I didn't kill her, Mike. Helen died a natural death. It was a mistake. That's all."

"I'm glad." His broad face was almost stern. "Lets have one last drink together, Harry," he said, "and then, I think it would be better if you did your drinking somewhere else."

"Sure, Mike. I understand."

He poured a jigger of gin for me and a short draught beer for himself. I downed the shot quickly, nodded briefly and left the bar. So Big Mike was glad. Everybody was glad, everybody was happy, everybody except me.

The overcast had yarded down thickly and now was a dark billowing fog. Soon it would drizzle, and then it would rain. I turned up my coat collar and put my head down. I didn't want to talk to anybody else. On my way to Mrs. McQuade's I had to pass several familiar places. The A & P, the Spotless Cleaners, Mr. Watson's delicatessen; all of these stores held people who knew me well. I pulled my collar up higher and put my head down lower.

When I reached the roominghouse I climbed the front outside steps and walked down the hall to Mrs. McQuade's door. I tapped twice and waited. As soon as she opened the door, Mrs. McQuade recognized me and clapped her hand to her mouth.

"It's quite all right, Mrs. McQuade," I said, "I'm a free man."

"Please come in, Mr. Jordan."

Her room was much too warm for me. I removed my jacket, sat down in a rocker and lighted one of my cigarettes to detract from the musty, close smell of the hot room. The old lady with blue hair sat down across from me in a straight-backed chair and folded her hands in her lap.

"It'll probably be in tonight's paper, Mrs. McQuade, but I didn't kill Helen. She died from a heart attack. A quite natural death. I didn't have anything to do with it."

"I'm not surprised." She nodded knowingly. "You both loved each other too much."

"Yes. We did."

Mrs. McQuade began to cry soundlessly. Her eyes searched the room, found her purse. She opened it and removed a Kleenex and blew her nose with a gentle, refined honk.

"How about Helen's things?" I asked. "Are they still here?"

"No. Her mother, Mrs. Mathews, took them. If I'd known that you . . . well, I didn't know, and she's Helen's mother, so when she wanted them, I helped her pack the things and she took them with her. There wasn't much, you know. That suitcase, now; I didn't know whether it was yours or Helen's so I let Mrs. Mathews take it."

"How about the portrait?"

"Mr. Endo was keeping it in his room. He wasn't here, but when she asked for it, I got it out of his room. She burned it up . . . in the incinerator. As I say, I didn't—"

"That's all right. I'd have liked to have had it, but it doesn't matter. Is there anything of hers at all?"

"Not a thing, Mr. Jordan. Just a minute." The old lady got out of her chair and opened the closet. She rummaged around in the small dark room. "These are yours." She brought forth my old trenchcoat and a gray laundry bag. I spread the trenchcoat on the floor and dumped the contents of the bag onto it. There were two dirty white shirts, four dirty T-shirts, four pairs of dirty drawers, six pairs of black sox and two soiled handkerchiefs.

At the bottom of the bag I saw my brushes and tubes of paint, and I could feel the tears coming into my eyes. She hadn't thrown them out after all; she still had had faith in me as an artist!

Mrs. McQuade pretended not to notice my choked emotion.

"If I'd known you were going to be released I'd have had these things laundered, Mr. Jordan."

"That's not important, Mrs. McQuade. I owe you some money, don't I?"

"Not a thing. Mrs. Mathews paid the room rent, and if you want the room you can have it back."

"No, thanks. I'm leaving San Francisco, I think it's best."

"Where are you going?"

"I don't know yet."

"Well, when you get settled, you'd better write me so I can forward your mail."

"There won't be any mail." I got out of the chair, slipped my jacket on, then the trenchcoat.

"You can keep that laundry bag, Mr. Jordan. Seeing I gave away your suitcase I can give you that much, at least."

"Thank you."

"Would you like a cup of coffee? I can make some in a second."

"No, thanks."

I threw the light bag over my shoulder and Mrs. McQuade opened the door for me. We shook hands and she led the way down the hall to the outside door. It was raining.

"Don't you have a hat, Mr. Jordan?"

"No. I never wear a hat."

"That's right. Come to think of it, I've never seen you with a hat."

I walked down the steps to the street and into the rain. A wind came up and the rain slanted sideways, coming down at an angle of almost thirty degrees. Two blocks away I got under the awning of a drug store. It wasn't letting up any; if anything, it was coming down harder. I left the shelter of the awning and walked up the hill in the rain.

Just a tall, lonely Negro.

Walking in the rain.

The End

About the Author

Charles Willeford was a professional horse trainer, boxer, radio announcer, and painter, as well as the author of over a dozen novels, including *The Burnt Orange Heresy, Pick-Up, Cockfighter*, and *Miami Blues*, a collection of short stories and a memoir of his war experiences. He was a tank commander with the Third Army in World War II. For his war efforts he received the Silver Star, the Bronze Star, the Purple Heart, and the Luxembourg Croix de Guerre. He also studied art in Biarritz, France, and in Lima, Peru, and English at the University of Miami. He died in 1988.